Lights Out, Slocum

Something struck Slocum and his world went black. He awoke sprawled on the ground, droplets striking his face. He realized they'd snuck up and knocked him out. *What about Meia?* The dark night felt empty, and his dull mind was pounded by a hard headache. He groped around in his black world. Found his sodden hat and put it on.

His rifle was gone. He moved to the bedroll—empty. That son of a bitch. Lost in the darkness, he vowed he'd get her back and make Arturo pay for all the pain he caused her.

JAKE LOGAN

SLOCUM
AND THE
MEDICINE MAN

JOVE BOOKS, NEW YORK

THE BERKLEY PUBLISHING GROUP
Published by the Penguin Group
Penguin Group (USA) Inc.
375 Hudson Street, New York, New York 10014, USA

Penguin Group (Canada), 90 Eglinton Avenue East, Suite 700, Toronto, Ontario M4P 2Y3, Canada
(a division of Pearson Penguin Canada Inc.)
Penguin Books Ltd., 80 Strand, London WC2R 0RL, England
Penguin Group Ireland, 25 St. Stephen's Green, Dublin 2, Ireland (a division of Penguin Books Ltd.)
Penguin Group (Australia), 250 Camberwell Road, Camberwell, Victoria 3124, Australia
(a division of Pearson Australia Group Pty. Ltd.)
Penguin Books India Pvt. Ltd., 11 Community Centre, Panchsheel Park, New Delhi—110 017, India
Penguin Group (NZ), 67 Apollo Drive, Rosedale, North Shore 0632, New Zealand
(a division of Pearson New Zealand Ltd.)
Penguin Books (South Africa) (Pty.) Ltd., 24 Sturdee Avenue, Rosebank, Johannesburg 2196,
South Africa

Penguin Books Ltd., Registered Offices: 80 Strand, London WC2R 0RL, England

This is a work of fiction. Names, characters, places, and incidents either are the product of the author's imagination or are used fictitiously, and any resemblance to actual persons, living or dead, business establishments, events, or locales is entirely coincidental.

SLOCUM AND THE MEDICINE MAN

A Jove Book / published by arrangement with the author

PRINTING HISTORY
Jove edition / September 2009

Copyright © 2009 by Penguin Group (USA) Inc.
Cover illustration by Sergio Giovine.

ISBN: 978-0-515-14692-9

JOVE®
Jove Books are published by The Berkley Publishing Group,
a division of Penguin Group (USA) Inc.
375 Hudson Street, New York, New York 10014.
JOVE® is a registered trademark of Penguin Group (USA) Inc.
The "J" design is a trademark of Penguin Group (USA) Inc.

PRINTED IN THE UNITED STATES OF AMERICA

10 9 8 7 6 5 4 3 2 1

Prologue

Afternoon storm clouds gathered in the west. A strong wind bore a wall of dust off the Dragoon Mountains and wrapped the skirt around the woman's calves. In the rush to recover the still-damp clothing off the line, she never even noticed the three Apaches sitting abreast on their paint ponies, watching her from behind some mesquite cover. Black streaks of war paint marked their faces, and beads of sweat gleamed on their bare bronze skin as they watched the handsome white woman struggle with her wash.

Long ago, the tip of a drunken Mexican's knife had ruined the leader's left eye. It had turned milky white, and the soldiers at San Carlos called him Snow Eye. A moniker that stuck to him both north and south of the border. The younger buck beside him was called Little Turkey. And No Pants made the third member of the small party that was out scouting for horses to steal. He'd earned his name escaping from an altercation in a wickiup with an angry husband in pursuit who had discovered him screwing his new bride. Their thoughts and plans at the moment centered on raping this white woman's ripe body to satisfy their strong hormonal needs. Each buck was ready to charge in and capture her, but Snow Eye held up an open hand to make them stay where they were.

"What is wrong?" Little Turkey asked as his anxious horse circled under him.

"Someone comes." Snow Eye tossed his head toward the south.

They turned to look for what he had noticed, while their ears listened to the rumble of the gathering storm.

"I hear only the thunder gods telling me she would be a fine one to stick my root into this day," No Pants said.

Snow Eye said, "Look there."

None of them had any problem seeing the two blue legs armed with repeaters, a white scout with them as they rode up to the woman.

"Keep your dick in your loincloth, No Pants. We better go back where we came from." He turned his pony around and the three headed into the face of the approaching storm.

"Who was that white scout with them?" Snow Eye asked over his shoulder.

"Slo-cum," No Pants said in disgust.

Little Turkey turned in the saddle and looked back, then booted his pony to catch up with them. Nodding his head to show that he knew the man, too, he said, "He is the one who Nadda says could screw a mare and make her smile."

"Nadda is a big whore. She likes any dick that's stuck in her. Who does he scout for?" Snow Eye asked.

No Pants shrugged. "I think he is a special scout for Natan Lupan."

"Hmm," Snow Eye snorted in disgust. "General Crook needs a special scout with all those traitors from our people that work for him? Why would he need a white man?"

Neither of them answered him, hurrying their ponies up the steep grade. Snow Eye looked back for the last time as they turned up the canyon and galloped into the mouth of the thunder god's fury. Cold hard rain began to pelt his bare skin.

White woman, you may have missed me having great pleasure with your body today, but I'll be back and do it twice as long. His coyote cries against the wall of the rain were ripped away by the roar of the storm.

1

"Let's go to the house and talk," Mrs. Ramsey said over the hard wind with her arms full of clothing. She knew one of the noncoms as Sergeant Harper, but the other one and the handsome white man she didn't know. The three men collected the rest of her wash, and joined her in the race for the clapboard residence.

Large drops began to fall on them before they reached her back porch and charged inside the house behind her. Out of breath, she piled her armful on the bed and hurried over to shut the back door. The handsome one reached past her and used his hand to help her force the door closed against the powerful force of the wind.

She looked up at him and felt something she seldom experienced when meeting a man's gaze. Her shoulders involuntarily shuddered under the ruffle-fronted dress, and goose bumps broke out on her arms.

"Strong wind," she said to him, wondering if the rest of him was like the broad shoulders and upper arms she could observe.

"Powerful, and it's a great shower—out there," he said.

Then, daring to steal one more look at this fascinating

man who smelled of rich leather and horse, she agreed and smiled. "Thanks for the help."

"They did it all." He indicated the two soldiers.

"Slocum, meet Mrs. Ramsey," the gray-headed Sergeant Harper said.

"Vanessa," she said, and offered Slocum her hand. And the son of a bitch kissed it. He could have shaken it or anything—but he firmly kissed it.

"My pleasure, Vanessa."

Her heart pounded under her breastbone. She hoped this man didn't know how much his presence upset her.

"This is Sergeant Mhoon from San Carlos," Harper said.

"Good day, sir, and thank you, too." She did a slight curtsy for the big hulking rawboned man with the large red nose. "Now the formalities are over, may I brew you gentlemen a cup of tea? I am afraid my libations are limited."

"Tea would be fine," Harper said, and the others agreed quickly.

"Have a seat at my table then." She indicated the ladderback chairs and swept around the room to bend over and stoke the cookstove. Fighting the strong desire to peek at this Slocum again, she deliberately kept her back to him while filling the kettle to heat the water in. Damn, if he did that to her while they were fighting a door shut, if they were left alone, they'd be screwing the hell out of one another inside of ten minutes.

"Captain Moore wants you to come to the camp," said Harper. "He's concerned for your safety out here alone."

She shook her head and did not turn. No way was she leaving this place—her place. Besides, Captain Moore was a wimp. Once, when they'd had the chance to do it, he'd spewed his cum all over her belly before he even started to put his dick inside her, and the second time he only lasted ten seconds. Who wanted to be around him? He'd pester her the whole time she stayed at the camp, promising her a better situation if she'd let him in her bed. She looked at the whitewashed ceiling boards for heavenly help. And here she was serving these men tea, even though her church thought tea to be the devil's brew.

"Mrs. Ramsey, this renegade Snow Eye and some others are off the reservation somewheres and he could show up here any day and time," Harper said with a fatherly concern in his voice.

"My husband, Onswell, is due back here in two weeks." After, of course, he made his rounds sleeping with all of his other wives en route and checking on their farming operations.

"That's a mighty long time to be out here alone." Harper shook his head ruefully.

Mhoon cleared his throat, but still started out in a raspy voice. "We can't haul you out of here, ma'am, but you need to listen to reason. Your husband might not get back here in time."

"For what, Sergeant?" she boldly asked him.

"Ah, ah, I mean—ma'am—them 'Paches don't do nice things to white women."

"These bronco Apaches are tough cold-blooded killers, Vanessa. They won't care who you are and won't have any respect for you," Harper said.

"But we've had this place for five years. All this time, they've only rode by and drank from my windmill tank."

"Different deal," Slocum said. "The old leaders are dead. Throwing all the Apaches together at San Carlos was like tying two cats by the tail and tossing them over a clothesline. Cats'll fight to the death of one or both of them. The one who can show the most damage to their enemies will be chosen the new leader of these rebels, and they'll flock to Mexico with him and build their numbers."

"I know some of them," she said. "Who are the ones competing for leadership?"

"The One Who Yawns is one," said Harper.

She nodded. "Geronimo. He once was married to Victorio's sister and the Mexicans killed her."

"Yes. Snow Eye is another. He's on the loose now."

"Is Geronimo on the loose, too?" she asked.

"No, he's been in irons. But if he gets the chance, he'll break out of San Carlos. You can't tell those hotshot Indian agents like Clum that putting those would-be leaders in irons only makes them harder to handle when they do release them. He thinks the opposite—that Geronimo'll be grateful to be free and fall in line."

"You think the army could handle them better than the Indian agent?" She cocked her head sideways to look back at Harper for his answer.

"I know we could," Harper said.

Staring directly at the quiet Slocum, she smiled. "Maybe they simply have the wrong men up there."

"Is that a question or a reply?" Slocum asked.

She turned around and dried her hands on a towel. "I have some peaches. May I open a can for you three? As for your question, Slocum, I'm not certain it isn't both."

He nodded at her. "I like the peaches idea the best."

She shared a private glance with him. He was obviously the toughest one of the three in her judgment, and the most appealing.

"We'd all like some of those peaches," Harper said.

Mhoon nodded his head as if impressed by her generosity.

The peaches she served the men in bowls proved to be sugar sweet and ripe. The steaming strong tea she poured into cups. Then she placed spoons and a small bowl of dark honey out for sweetener.

"Mrs. Ramsey, my orders are to bring you back to Camp Fork until this renegade crisis lets up."

"Sergeant Harper, I appreciate your concern for my welfare, but these people have left me alone up until now. I will simply have to take my chances."

"I'd hate to have to come up here and bury your corpse, ma'am."

Her chin rose proudly, and she shook her head to dismiss his concern. "I wouldn't care. I guess I'd be dead. No, I'm not leaving at this time."

"Gentlemen, I guess we aren't going to convince this lady to leave," Slocum said, looking for their response.

"Thank you, Slocum," she said. Already, she liked him. Not only his appearance appealed to her, but he sounded like a man who thought about lots of things. Educated—that must be it. An officer dressed in a buckskin shirt—part savage, the other half upper-class society.

She'd give a pretty polished penny to know his history. How many women he'd slept with, and made cry when he rode off. Oh, he was the heartbreaking kind all right, and looked like he had the stamina and training to make a woman smile when he finished with her, too.

Who was he? Why was he scouting for the army? A lowly job for man of his caliber. All questions she'd like to know as the saliva gathered in her mouth at the thought of kissing him and then being screwed to death on her bed. Oh, God, grant me that wish—one time anyway.

When the storm was over, after thanking her, and re-signed to her wish to remain there, the three men rode out and passed eastward toward the Chiricahuas to gather other women and children off their isolated ranches and farms. Slocum had raised his hat and smiled at her with the confidence of a man who knew how she thought. It was a private smile simply for her. She felt her face flush. He'd be back for her, and the notion of their next meeting made her cheeks turn hot.

Damn, Slocum, who are you?

Hours later that night, from a deep sleep while lying in her bed, her eyes flew open with a start. Someone was in-side her house. Earlier, the night wind had died down, and now she could hear her intruder's breathing over the crick-ets. Not daring to move and let the invader know she wasn't asleep, she could feel every palpation of her heart. The raw musk of the invader soon filled her nostrils. Her stomach began to crawl. This was not a white man.

When he put his knee on the bed and swept the sheet away, her breath caught in her throat. His hard, calloused hand rolled her over on her back and he loomed above her. Panic seized her racing heart—but she mustn't scream. That would only encourage a savage.

In the room's dim light, with him kneeling above her, she could look down and see his huge waving wand. He forced her nightgown up her legs into a wad at her waist. Everything from that moment on felt like a dream to her. The cool night air sought the exposed skin on her legs and lower belly.

"Ah," he grunted, spreading her legs apart and moving in position to stab his huge dick inside her.

At his not-too-gentle entry, she wanted to cry out, but cut the sound off in her throat. From his intrusion, she realized how powerful he must be. His slender body felt like a rawhide quirt handle, hard-braided but still limber enough to be flexible. Soon, her body became a traitor to her. The hard pumping action with his stiff prick's friction on the walls and her rising clit began to arouse her to new heights of dazzling excitement.

Her breath soon became short, and this forced her to open her mouth to suck for air. She tossed her head on the mattress, and her hair soon covered her face.

From deep in his throat, the primal growls began to roar. He was seeking relief. Instinctively, she raised her legs and clasped them around him, letting him go even deeper. The walls of her vagina began to swell and contract. They both sounded like runaway huffing steam engines in their fight for relief. At last, he arched his back and shoved his erection in as deep as it could go. After some pained straining by both of them, she felt his hot fountain of sperm exploding inside her—*then she fainted*.

2

Naco, the Chiricahua scout, squatted in his knee-high raw-hide boots. The way he searched the ground for signs satisfied Slocum. The short Apache with the dutch-bob haircut and red headband was appraising the situation in the dirt outside Mrs. Ramsey's house.

"Where did she go?" Slocum asked, stepping off the porch and heading for Naco. "Maybe better yet, who took her?"

"She and an Apache left here last night." Naco held up a brown finger to indicate there was only one Apache.

Slocum looked off at the towering Chiricahua Mountains on the east side of the Sulfur Springs Valley. "The house is not torn up. She may have taken some things in a bundle. The top sheet that was on the bed is gone, and maybe a few things missing that a white woman would take. The mirror and brush are not there."

"If she took that, maybe she went with him," the scout said.

"I could tell you what they'll say about that at the fort."

Naco twisted around on his toes to look toward him. "What is that?"

11

"White women would never run off with savages. They are always abducted against their will."

Naco laughed. "Who was that captain's wife at Fort Apache who ran off with that young buck up there?"

"Oh, no," Slocum said mockingly. "It was the boy who abducted her, and the troopers shot him up on the Rio Salado and brought her back safely."

Naco laughed. "Why was she always red-eyed after that from crying for him?"

"Don't know that, but I guess when we get back, we better tell Captain Moore that the Apaches got Mrs. Ramsey."

"What next?"

"Where did he go with her?"

"Up in the Dragoons, I guess." Naco gave a head toss in that direction.

"Willing or unwilling, we better go see if we can find her."

Naco nodded, and in a bound was in the Western saddle on the sorrel gelding the army had issued him. Slocum unhitched the big dun and stepped aboard. Moments later, they were headed up the deep canyon behind her place. Naco bent over reading sign on the ground until he acted certain, and then he sat up in the saddle. With a nod, he hurried on ahead.

A good Apache tracker could follow a pissant over rocks. From an early age, they learned how to track, and the older they became, the keener they were at it. In fact, Slocum believed it was a psychic power they were born with.

The horses of Slocum and Naco scrambled atop the loose gravel on the steep trail. The lip above them looked only yards away but when they reached it, the way opened to reveal more of the face of the mountain that had to be climbed.

"They had been watching her," Naco said.

Slocum frowned at the scout ahead of him and gave his horse more rein. "How do you know that?"

"There were piles of horse shit down there above the house in a mesquite grove. It was Indian horse shit. No grain. Lots of mesquite bean seeds in it. They'd sat their ponies and watched her from there."

"How many?"

"Maybe three." He held up his fingers as their grunting animals fought the harsh slope and loose footing. Then he gave a head toss toward the top. "We are about there."

"Good."

"You know this woman?" Naco asked.

"I only met her one day and ate her peaches."

Naco laughed. "All you did was meet her and eat her peaches?"

"Yeah, Sergeant Harper and Mhoon were along."

"I see. I know the Apaches used her water tank—she never seemed to mind. It was good water and when the windmill ran, the drink from the pipe was real cool."

"That's why she felt they wouldn't bother her." Slocum wondered what Naco's answer would be.

"Her peace treaty might not have been with all the Apaches. Just some."

"I savvy that."

At last, they reined up on top of the slope, and the rush of cooler air swept over Slocum's sweaty face. He could look down in the deep canyon choked with live oak and some cedars and be grateful to be on top.

"You ever see her?" Slocum asked.

"A few times, but I'd heard of her and her water. She was a Mormon?"

"Captain Moore said she was. Said her husband was a polygamist who had several wives on different farms and ranches. He drove a buckboard, went by, and caught up the heavy chores at each one. She expected him in a week or so to be by her place."

Naco nodded. "Let's go find them."

"They close by here?"

"Maybe in the next canyon. There is water there." He

twisted in the saddle and looked back as they started out again. "Where are her children?"

"She's had none, according to Moore."

"I saw her at the camp once, maybe twice. She was a tall good-looking woman. Moore chased her like a bitch in heat." Naco grinned back at Slocum.

"I don't blame him. I would, too."

They both laughed.

In a short while, they were off the ridge and in a grove of live oak trees. Naco made a sign to dismount and Slocum agreed.

"Sounds carry in these canyons. I don't want them to hear us coming. We better go on foot from here."

The horses hitched, they took the Winchesters out of their scabbards, and Naco set out in a long trot. Slocum knew the scout wanted to look things over. By himself, he could do it quieter than the two of them. His red headband soon disappeared on the game trail going down into the canyon. There was good cover under the canopy of the oaks and a small trickle of water in the draw. Slocum moved downhill as quiet and observant as he could be, occasionally stopping when threatened by the shrill mimicked calls of the Mexican mockingbird. Smiling at the brash bird's twirling copycat notes, he went on.

A mile or so down the mountainside, he spotted his scout squatted with his back to a gnarled tree trunk. The rifle lay across his knees. Slocum joined him and did the same with his weapon.

"Find 'em?"

"Me find 'em." Naco nodded matter-of-factly. "But I didn't see her."

"You think she's around? Or they killed her?"

He gave a head toss toward the west. "We can go ask them."

"Fine, let's do that."

The camp was made of two wikiups. Apache lodges never impressed Slocum like the Plains Indians' tepees and lodges had. The Apache lodges were made of brush and dead sticks, with some old canvas on the top to shed the occasional rain.

Three horses raised up their heads, and then two bucks came outside. Slocum wondered if the Apaches had noticed their own horses' behavior. The two Indians in camp looked surprised as Naco stood before them with his rifle leveled at the pair.

"Who are they?" Slocum asked, looking around for more Apaches and the Ramsey woman. He found no one in either of the brush lodges.

"One is No Pants and the other is Little Turkey." Naco motioned at them with his rifle's muzzle. "Where is Ojo Nevado?"

Slocum knew that was Snow Eye's Spanish name.

They shrugged. At last, the one Naco called Little Turkey said, "He has been gone all day and night, too."

Naco shook his head with an angry scowl written on his hard face. "No, you lie to me. He and the woman came here earlier."

Little Turkey showed some fear. "No."

"Tell me where he is or I'll take your head back to San Carlos in a sack."

"They went to the mother mountains. I swear. He said to tell no one."

Naco still looked undecided about the truth, "Why didn't you two go with him?"

Little Turkey looked at Slocum first and then, as if satisfied the big white man was not going to explode, he spoke. "He did not wish us along. I think he wanted a honeymoon."

"Where were you to meet him?"

"In ten days on the Rio Blanco, and to bring ten more men."

"Well, you two are going back to San Carlos so you won't meet him down there that quick." Naco turned back to Slocum. "You hear him? He took her to the Sierra Madres."

"For a honeymoon, huh?" Slocum laughed at the notion. "Maybe we shouldn't tell Captain Moore?"

"Him and the rest of them officers wouldn't believe us anyway." Naco laughed about it as he herded the bucks to get their horses for the ride back to the camp.

The two bucks, with their hands tied behind their backs, were tossed on their saddles, and each horse was on a lead rope and Naco led them in a line. The third horse came after that. Slocum rode in the rear as the guard.

After midnight, they arrived at the row of sidewall tents on the San Pedro River, a shallow desert stream that almost dried up between very occasional heavy monsoon rains. Camp Fork was a temporary post twenty miles from Fort Huachuca. The night guard challenged them on their approach.

"Scout Slocum and Naco with two prisoners." He pushed his horse on by the man.

"Well, Slocum, you mean them red devils ain't roasted your balls yet?"

"No. And another thing, Private Larsen. They ain't going to either."

Larsen laughed. "Them sons a bitches will get your ass. You just wait and see."

"I don't like him," Naco said, riding in beside Slocum.

"That's nothing new," Slocum said in a soft voice. "No one else does either."

Naco nodded.

The officer in charge came out of the lamp-lit operations tent while buttoning his coat.

"Lieutenant Scopes, sir," Slocum said to the man. "We have two renegades for you."

"I see that. Fine job. Where did you find them?"

"Dragoons. They say Snow Eye cut out for Mexico with Mrs. Ramsey."

"Oh, how horrible. That poor woman. She was a very nice lady. I am saddened to hear that. Private Luther, you and three men take those two prisoners and chain them for the night."

"Yes, sir."

"Slocum, come in and we'll fill out a report."

"You have any food, Lieutenant?"

"Oh, you two haven't eaten?"

"Not lately."

"Excuse me, we can go down to the mess tent and stir up someone."

"That sounds better."

"Luther, see to their horses, too."

"Yes, sir."

The noncom cook they stirred up growled like a bear when they woke him. But in a short time, skillets scraped on the iron-top field stoves, and the smell of burning mesquite and oak soon filled the air as Slocum gave his report.

"Snow Eye is in Mexico?"

"Sierra Madres, if you can believe them," Slocum said.

"What do you think, Naco?" Scopes asked.

The scout nodded matter-of-factly. "He probably went there."

"My God, that poor woman is right now, while we speak, being raped and abused all that long way down there." Scopes shook his head in disbelief. "It makes my blood boil to think that savage son of a bitch took her out of her comfortable way of life and is using her body like some—like some whore in the dirt."

"We got up to her place too late," Slocum said, nodding to the cook, who served him and Naco each a heaping tin plate of German fried potatoes and onions with three fried eggs apiece.

"Damn good food, thanks," Slocum said after his first bite while the man refilled his coffee cup.

Naco waved his fork at him. "Best food I ate today."

"It's the only food you had all fucking day long," the cook said, and laughed.

"Maybe."

"Lieutenant, after this, I'm going to sleep about twenty-four hours," Slocum said, and went back to work on his plate. "And then I'll see what Captain Moore wants us to do about her. If anything."

The fresh West Pointer drew in a deep breath. "I am certain the captain will want something done about it, but I don't know what we can do. General Crook hasn't got the details worked out yet for us to go across the border in pursuit of those troublemakers."

"Tell Moore not to wake me for twenty-four hours any way that goes," Slocum said.

"I will, but you know Captain Moore."

He knew the sumbitch well, but if Moore knew what was good for him, he'd better let him sleep.

3

She stood waist-deep in the rushing cold water. From behind, her lover cupped her firm pear-shaped breasts and shoved his half erection against her tight butt. She closed her eyes to savor his attention. Bone-tired from the long days in the saddle and the arduous nights full of his ferocious lovemaking, she felt dizzy as his strong, calloused hands moved over her smooth skin. He nibbled her ear and rubbed his palm over her mound, teasing her crack as he searched it with his fingers.

Setting her feet apart, she wondered if he wanted—how he could want her again so soon? But she knew from the growing stiffness behind her—he would not want to wait long either. Oh, my God—she couldn't believe it, but it would soon be so.

Sweeping the hair back from her eyes, she looked at the towering Madres that surrounded them. This place must be heaven, and he was the answer she never knew existed for the powerful, demanding needs she felt so often between her legs. Then, without warning, he swept her up in his arms and waded for the shore. They could take a bath anytime—he had more important things to do to her. *Oh, my God.*

Captain Moore's face looked chiseled out of stone. Straight-backed as most cavalry officers were, he sat up in the canvas chair and flopped the riding quirt around on the desktop. "So this fucking Snow Eye took her?"

"I'm not sure about that part, but he did, by those bucks' words, take the lady to Mexico," said Slocum.

"You know damn good and well what that savage is doing to her."

"I can guess. But you have no authority down there."

"Ramsey will be up here when he hears about it, demanding that we do something."

"Nothing you can do. He'll just have to wait it out."

"A good man and a couple of ex-army scouts could go down there and get her out." Moore slapped at a fly on his desk with the quirt and killed it.

"Not me. Besides, I have to go meet General Crook in three days."

"I could send him a message by courier that you had to go off and see about the renegades that were reported to you."

Slocum shook his head. "No, I have to make an oral report to the commander."

"Did we pass your inspection down here?"

Slocum nodded. "You and your men sure try. It's a vast land and a cagey enemy."

"Really, what can we do about Mrs. Ramsey?"

"Captain Moore, I have no idea. She should have come out when the two noncoms and I went over and asked her to. She wouldn't come, and Snow Eye came back for her."

"Came back?"

"Yes, Naco said they'd been up in the brush watching her. They may have even been out there the day we went to see her. No doubt waiting for a chance to catch her."

"I don't know what I'll tell her husband. Poor man will be beside himself."

"Yeah, he doesn't have over a half dozen more wives."

"That's his religion."

"I'm not arguing. I'll take Naco with me. You have four scouts."

"Lazy, but four on the pay roster." Moore made a disgusted face.

"I'll tell Crook to switch them out. They get under Tom Horn, he'll ride the britches off them."

"If he can get them to move."

"Hell, Horn will or know why." Slocum stood up. "We can make Bowie before they close the mess hall tonight if we ride hard. I'm sorry we did not save her, but we got you two runaways anyway."

"Yes, that was a good deal. Ride careful."

The two shook hands and Slocum went outside the tent, where Naco squatted in the shade. Slocum gave the scout a head toss. They mounted up and rode out.

The push was hard. They bypassed the silver mining boomtown of Tombstone, crossed the Sulfur Springs Valley, and swung around the base of the Chiricahuas so that at sundown, they watered their done-in horses at Apache Springs and rode on in. The mess hall was closed, but the officer in charge sent for food for them.

Lieutenant Moates acted excited to see them and to learn about their capture of the two renegades. "Was this Ojo Nevado with them?"

"No, he's the one we think kidnapped Mrs. Ramsey."

Moates slapped his forehead. "What a gorgeous woman. You think that shaman has her?"

"He left with her. She may be dead right now."

"Oh, what a shame. That damn Apache may have screwed her to death."

Slocum shook his head. It would have taken more than one buck, no matter how endowed he was, to have screwed that woman to death. Every officer he'd spoken to about her, from Moore on down, acted like they'd been fascinated by her. Nice body, but maybe he'd missed all of that, or maybe he hadn't been isolated from women as long as some of them.

Plates of food were delivered, and Slocum filled his own tin cup from the headquarters water barrel to wash down the biscuits and beef stew. Naco sat cross-legged on the floor to eat. Slocum used Moates's desk.

"Well, you made it back," the gruff-voiced Crook said, entering the log building with a cigar in his hand. "You all right, Naco?"

"Fine, now I can eat."

"Both of you go ahead. As you were, Moates." Crook pulled up a canvas folding chair and sat down by Slocum.

"How are we doing?" Crook asked.

Slocum looked over at him. "We win some. We lose some. Captain Moore needs some fresh scouts down on the San Pedro."

"Fresh scouts, huh?"

"Assign those down there to Horn. They need to get off their ass."

Naco agreed with a nod.

"What else?" asked Crook.

"A renegade called Ojo Nevado by the Mexicans kidnapped a Mrs. Ramsey, who lived on a ranch over by the Dragoons a few days ago, and lit out for the Sierra Madres with her."

"Snow Eye," Crook said, and shook his head. "He's one of those fortune-tellers. A shaman. I think he could be real trouble if he ever gets a band going. In the past, the whole damn bunch were controlled by Cochise, but since he died, they splintered up. We don't need this medicine man reviving Cochise's role, or we'll never keep them at San Carlos and Fort Apache."

"You think he's that powerful?" Slocum wondered why Crook was so concerned about a one-eyed buck who'd run off with a Mormon's wife.

"Moates, send someone for Tom Horn. If he's sober, have him come up here. Al Sieber was worried about Snow

Eye. Al's gone to Preskitt, something about some problems with the scouts at Camp Verde."

The biscuits were cold and dry. But Slocum sopped them up in the stew juice and ate them with a fork. Crook took out a bottle of whiskey, and Slocum downed his water before he let the general pour whiskey in his mug.

Moates found Naco and the general a cup each to use, and then he took the bottle to set it on the desk.

"Here's to your health," Crook said, and toasted the two of them. "And may these Apaches all die of old age on the reservation."

Bare-headed, Tom Horn walked into the room. Not a tall man, of slender build, he moved like a mountain lion, muscled and lithe on his feet. He looked bright, and smiled at Slocum and Naco when he saw them. "General, you wanted me?"

"They got close to Snow Eye over in the Dragoons. I was telling them you and Al are concerned about him," Crook said.

"How close?" Horn frowned hard at them.

"A few hours maybe," said Slocum. "We arrested a young buck called Turkey and another named No Pants."

"Where did Ojo Nevado go after that?"

"Naco and I think he kidnapped Mrs. Ramsey, a rancher's wife over by the Dragoons, and headed out for the Madres with her."

"Vanessa," Horn said softly, pulling up another chair. "You meet her?"

"Yes, I rode up there with two sergeants to try and get her to go to Camp Fork until this Apache uprising lets up. Nice lady."

Horn leaned back and gazed at the ceiling, rubbing his neck, and then he straightened and ruefully shook his head. "Where was he headed?"

"Rio Blanco. He told his men to meet him up there."

"Well—" Horn looked over at Crook, and when the general nodded, he went on. "Al Sieber and I learned from a scout named Hieko that this Snow Eye was at a *tiswin* party and told Geronimo that Clum was going to put him in chains. Told him who would arrest him, named the four Indian police and what time and day they would come for him.

"You know, Geronimo is quite a fortune-teller, too. He scoffed at Snow Eye, and by God, it happened just like Snow Eye said to the nickel."

"I guess the rest up there took heed of his prophecy, huh?" Slocum asked.

Horn shook his head in defeat, then swiped his hair back from his forehead. "It could be a real mess. All them bucks are looking for one sign. That was good enough to set something else up. We thought he already was in Mexico, or at least that's what my scouts figured."

"No, he was in the Dragoons. Turkey told Naco that Snow Eye told them before he left that camp to go get ten men from San Carlos and meet him in Mexico."

"General," Horn said. "We don't get permission to cross that border soon, he may boil up a mess them Mexicans will regret forever."

"That's in the hands of the State Department. They don't want another damn war with Mexico."

"Hell, take them buffalo soldiers cavalry down at Huachuca and give them baseball bats and point them in the direction of Mexico City. Why, they could whip ass on the whole Mexican army."

"If it was that easy, I'd do it. But you and I know the reason Congress did not buy the northern half of Mexico when they had the chance and Mexico was willing to sell it, and Baja as well. They didn't want any more brown skins than they had, and Catholics to boot. They still don't want them."

"Well, hell, how can you wage a war with your hands tied?" Horn said in disgust.

"It won't be easy." Crook turned to Slocum. "Could you

and Naco slip down there and see what's going on? Say, you as a rancher and him as your guide? I couldn't offer you any protection. The Mexican army, if they catch you, might even consider you a spy."

"All you'd like is the information on him?" Slocum asked.

"Yes, if he's doing anything down there to raise an army, I need to know what it is. I'd also really like that lady brought back if she's still alive. I could say the army saved her, huh?"

"We'll look for her, but we can't promise anything."

"Just do your best."

Slocum agreed that he would.

"I want to warn you that Who and his band are also down there in the Madres," Horn said. "He's a bloody bastard. Watch out for him. His band stays down there, but they've made some raids up here with the Chiricahuas. Snow Eye might be going to join up with him."

"Sounds like a great place to be," Slocum said, shaking his head and smiling in defeat.

Horn agreed. "Ah, a nice lot of bloodthirsty bastards."

"Are you're willing to go down there to look the situation over and report back?" Crook asked. "And do what you can about her?"

"Yes, I'll try, but not a word to any of the other scouts," Slocum said. "Word travels fast enough."

"I agree," Horn said. "You're never sure who you can trust in this game."

"When're you going to leave?" Crook asked.

"When's the stage to Lordsburg leave the Apache Pass Station?"

"In the morning," Moates said.

"How early?"

"Five to six A.M. or so."

"I'll be on it and so will Naco."

"Why Lordsburg?" Crook asked with a frown.

"Catch some freight wagons or some miners there going

into Mexico and ride along with them if we can find someone. It would make better cover than if him and I go down across south of here."

"Good idea," Crook agreed. "Be careful. You'll need some money. Captain Booner can issue that. Moates, send for him."

Slocum shook Tom's calloused hand. The hardest hand he could recall on any man. "Thanks. Good to see you again."

"Yeah, always. You find Mrs. Ramsey, tell her I sent my best to her."

Slocum looked around and saw that Crook was over talking to Moates, so he turned back to Horn. "You ever hop in her bed?"

"She was sure sweet hot stuff." Horn shook his head like he really regretted she wasn't there.

"I'll give her your regards if I find her."

"Do that, hoss. See you." Horn winked at him, then told the general good night and left.

Captain Booner soon arrived. Crook told him what Slocum needed. The officer went and took five hundred dollars from the safe. He counted it out in Slocum's hand. "Good luck on your mission."

Another shot of Crook's bottle, a handshake with the general for good luck, and Slocum headed with Naco for the scout camp. A clear picture of the straight-backed old warhorse in his near-civilian clothing that evening remained in Slocum's mind. Crook was tough as that mule called Apache that he rode.

"You got a bedroll?" Naco asked when they reached the area near the spring.

"No. I need to get one, I guess."

"I'll find you one. Wait here." Naco took off in the night.

Under the stars, close to a thick walnut tree that had survived many floods down this dry wash, he listened to the crickets play. The heat of the day was fast evaporating. In the distance, a dog barked, and soon Naco returned with a short Apache woman wrapped in a blanket that covered her head.

"Josie here has a blanket for both of you. Should I awaken you before sunrise?"

"Yes, we have a stage to catch."

Naco nodded and left them. The short woman shook free of the cover and tossed her head toward the west. "We go there. No one bother us."

"Fine," he said, and walked behind her. In the moonlight, she looked young and not ugly. In a grove of juniper, she unfurled a second blanket she had carried under her arm. She spread it on the ground, nodded at him, and began to untie her many skirts.

He toed off his boots, took off his gun belt, and shed his pants, which he hung on a bough. She sat naked on the pallet and waited for him to join her. The starlight shone on her small pointed breasts. He put the revolver and holster close by where his head would be and lay down on his back gazing at the million stars in the galaxy.

With the large robe over them, she rolled against him and threw her arm on his stomach. "You plenty big man."

She was plenty small, but he didn't say that. "Big enough for you?"

A giggle escaped her mouth. Indian women giggled like little girls when faced with serious things. It must be a way to relieve their tension. Her small fingers sought his genitals. Then gently, she began to jack off his half erection.

Raising half up, she frowned at him. "How big does he get?"

"About that size."

She nodded. "He be plenty big. We better try him now."

He raised up and she scooted under him. With her legs spread wide beneath him, he felt like he towered over her like a stud horse screwing a pony mare. She inserted him with both hands, and he eased it in and out of her wet gates. She arched her back and hunched her butt toward him as he sought to go deeper and deeper inside her. Soon, they were in the wild free spin of unbridled passion, with him pumping her for all he was worth.

Her moans of pleasure grew louder and louder. The walls of her vagina swelled, making it tighter and tighter for his entry. Her clit raked the top of his erection like a nail. They were locked in a flight of fire that consumed both of them.

His breath rushed through his throat, and then he felt two arrows pierce his ass. He shoved hard into her and stayed tight. The rise of his semen from his testicles took flight like a rocket and exploded out the head of his swollen dick. Not once, but twice, he came hard, and she collapsed in a pile under him like melted ice tossed out on a hot desert.

"Holy day, where do you live?" she mumbled, sounding drunk, sprawled on her back as if he'd shot her.

"Where do you sleep?"

"Here with you tonight." She snuggled against him.

"I mean where do you live?"

"Under those stars above us. You got a wife?"

"No."

"You need one, you come find me. Josie Little Horse. I make you plenty good one."

He kissed her on the mouth and her eyes flew open in shock. "Why do that?"

"'Cause you're sweet."

She squirmed her firm body against him. "You a plenty good big sumbitch."

"I better sleep."

"You sleep." She put her folded hands under her face with her rock hard small butt wiggled against his belly.

He closed his eyes and wondered about Mrs. Ramsey and if she'd even survived for this long. Then he slept.

4

Ojo Nevado had been gone for a day. Mrs. Ramsey carried a large bundle of dead sticks slung over her shoulder to make small cooking fires with. Apaches could dig a hole with a big knife to build a fire in, then cook in a vessel over it, and not let hardly any smoke escape for their enemies to sniff on the wind.

The days on the desert crossing had turned her face tan despite the wide hat she wore. And her hands looked as dark as his—good thing she did not burn like most white women. The color did not bother her. The shunning of women in their menstruation was something she needed to get used to. She couldn't expose him—that would be severe bad luck for him, he said. But her time was over for another few weeks.

It was different to be the hunted. Twice, they snuck by the Mexican army's camps, so close they could hear the men snoring. Then rode on all night and in the daytime they hid in some abandoned hacienda. There had once been many palatial estates in the desert, but Apache raiders had forced the hacienda owners to flee to Mexico City to save their lives and wives.

Ojo told her about the raids. They must have taken place when the Apaches were more numerous. She had only seen two bucks since leaving the Dragoons. That was at a water hole. They were going back to the reservation to and try to find new wives. Some Mexican scalpers had killed their women and children to collect the bounty on their hair.

She felt sorry for them. They were young men barely in their twenties. Ojo explained that times were hard for his people, but soon they would all gather in the Madres and again show their strength to the Mexican army and then the Americans. The Mexicans he had no concern over fighting. The Americans, he knew, would require a large force to take them on. But in the end, the land that was the Apaches' would be theirs again.

Stopped on a hillside to catch her breath, she put her hand on her hips and smiled. What would Onswell Ramsey think when he drove up to her place with a big hard-on in his pants and nothing to stick it into? She laughed out loud at the notion of his despair, and then shifted the load on her back.

A horse was coming. Good. He'd be real horny after being away from her for so long.

Slocum and Naco climbed in the stage with the dim light of morning glinting off the mountaintop above them. It was early. The fresh horses stomped impatiently, making the harness chains jingle. The station man closed the coach door behind them.

"They're in, Chuck," he shouted to the driver.

The predawn chill of the desert swept in the coach at the first lurch. Slocum could regret leaving his jumper tied on behind the saddle under the tarp in back. Wedged in beside a large man who smelled strongly of whiskey and snored like a hog, he nodded to Naco. The young woman seated next to his scout was behind a veil that covered her face, and was turned away toward the window, snuggled in her corner, feigning asleep. She also wore a long black silk coat that wrapped her like a cocoon.

The sun was up by the time they reached the next stage stop out on the playas. The wide lakes that covered many acres looked like an ocean in the midst of the desert, when they actually were only inches deep. Many a land swindle had been made pretending the lakes were water sources to irrigate with. He climbed down, then aided the woman, who was forced to raise her veil to see how to get down.

Thin-faced, with large dark eyes, she wasn't as ugly as he'd guessed her to be, though she was a little older. Close to thirty or thirty-five. She thanked him coldly, and headed for the outhouse the driver had mentioned when he stopped. *The facilities are in back*, he'd said. Naco joined Slocum, and the bear of a drunk came out of the stage last, growling and falling to his knees. They ignored him.

After using the outhouse, the two stepped out of the stinky confines, and the lady in black with her nose in the air went past them as if anxious to escape everything— them included.

"Hello, darling." The drunk doffed his hat and blocked her way.

"Stand aside," she said, trying to go around him.

"Why, me darling—" The sight of the gun in Slocum's hand behind her made his face flush.

"Stand aside for her," Slocum ordered.

She nodded to Slocum and hurried on.

When Slocum was satisfied she was beyond hearing, he spoke sharply to the man. "You have bad bowel problems. Stay in those facilities until the stage leaves. I'll have the driver set off your things."

"There's nothing wrong with my—"

"There will be if you don't do as I say. Stay in that shit-house until the stage leaves, or my Apache friend here will stake you out on an anthill."

Naco nodded that he would do that.

"I—I—"

"You hear me?"

"Yes, yes, I will." His hands, held shoulder high, were trembling and his flabby double chin shaking. "Don't shoot."

Slocum waved him inside. Then he and Naco went around in front where the driver with the handlebar mustache was sucking on a toothpick with his shoulder against a porch support.

"The man traveling with us wishes his bags set off. He has bowel problems and won't be able to continue with us."

Chuck half suppressed a grin. "I can do that."

They rolled across the desert for Lordsburg in the warming sun. Slocum, Naco, and Mrs. Culmeyer. She said she was going to San Antonio to see about her ailing mother.

"There is rail service from Lordsburg on," she said.

Slocum nodded. "I guess you will be relieved to at last be on those tracks and off this rocking coach?"

"I have a layover in Lordsburg tonight. I arranged my trip because these stages are so undependable and I didn't want to miss my train."

"Is there anyone to show you around in Lordsburg?"

"No. Are you familiar with this outpost?"

"I know it. Kind of a rough place, being the end of the tracks and all."

"Since you so graciously saved me from Mr. Prior, perhaps you could show me around, sir?"

"I imagine I could, ma'am. My name's Slocum and that's Naco."

"Nice to meet you both. You have business in Lordsburg?" She crossed her legs and straightened her stiff skirt.

"No, we're going to Mexico to look at some mining and ranching ventures."

"Isn't that dangerous? I understand the Apaches are marauding in the north of Mexico, and there are bandits, too."

"That's why Naco's along. He's an Apache and my guide."

"I see. You're a resourceful man, Mr. Slocum." Her smile was warm as the mid-morning sun.

After the next stage stop, she was sitting beside Slocum, telling him all about the ranch in California. They grew dates, figs, lemons, and oranges, and also ran cattle in the desert. Her husband had found enough gold in the rush era to start his holdings, and was older than her by twenty years. She'd come out there from Texas to teach school, and he'd swept her off her feet. Aside from the fact they'd never had any children, she lived the serene social life of a wife with a very rich husband.

Naco was asleep on the other seat when she reached up with her gloved hand and steadied Slocum's face. She rose up enough to move her pursed mouth toward his. Her eyes closed under the long black lashes when he kissed her; he knew how a bee felt sipping nectar from a flower.

Then, with her back nestled against him and his arms around her, she smiled. "I don't think the layover I've been dreading will be so bad after all."

"No, Mrs. Culmeyer, I don't think it will be."

"Leona," she quietly corrected him. "And since my hotel room is reserved in my dear husband's name, and they have never seen him and will never see him, this evening you shall be Hubert Culmeyer when we check in, if that is all right?"

"Good enough—Leona, my dear."

She snuggled against him. "I never thought I'd meet a man such as you in my travels."

"You never can tell."

"No." She put his arms around her as if to hide inside them. "It is the first time on this trip I have felt truly safe and not had my hand in my purse, holding the grip of the Ladysmith .22."

They both laughed.

The stage arrived in bustling Lordsburg in the late afternoon. Train whistles blew and switch engines screeched up and down the sidings, shuffling cars around. Naco took charge of their saddles and things, and promised Slocum he'd be around Nelson's Livery if Slocum needed him.

"I'll see you in the morning," Slocum said softly to the scout. Naco nodded that he understood.

At the Congress Hotel, the desk clerk immediately acknowledged him as Mr. Culmeyer. "So glad to have you here, sir, and you, too, ma'am."

"If you have our luggage taken upstairs to our room, the Missus and I shall go find some supper."

"That will be handled, sir."

"Good."

They found a café down the street and a vacant table. He put her chair under her, and then removed his hat to set it on an empty chair. Her eyes were the color of coal and they sparkled looking at him.

"He did think you were Hubert." Wrapped up in her black coat, she huddled inside it like a cocoon as she looked both amused and attractive to him.

"He had no doubts." His hand reached across the table and she hesitated for a moment, then put her own hand out for him to squeeze. "I am going to take you back after this meal, and order you a bath in the room—then slip out and get one myself and a shave. I want nothing to disturb this evening."

Her eyes widened and then she smiled, pleased. "How nice and considerate of you."

"Well, we have sliced roast beef, mashed potatoes, gravy, and green beans on the plate meal," the wide-hipped waitress said, standing over them.

When he glanced over at Leona, she nodded in approval. "Sounds good. Coffee for me—" he said.

"Coffee will be all right," Leona said.

"Coming right up," the woman said, and sashayed off.

"I really dreaded this night the most," she said, wrapping the coat around her like she was cold. "Alone and being in a strange frontier town. A place I'd never been except passing through on a stage before the railroad even got this far. I had dreaded this night so much. And now it turns out so well."

"I'm looking forward to it."

She blushed and averted her eyes. "You will have to be patient with me. I am not learned at—at this."

"No problem."

After the meal, they went back to the hotel. At the desk, he ordered her up a tub and hot water. Then he showed her to the room. He went to the window and looked down on the busy street. Better go see about getting himself cleaned up. From halfway across the room, she came at him open-armed and hugged him. Resting her cheek on his chest, she squeezed him tight.

"I'll be waiting," she said in a whisper.

"So will I." He used his fist under her chin to raise her face and kissed her softly.

The bathhouse business was slow that evening. The Chinese man showed him to the tub, and two small women dressed in kimonos and wooden sandals brought in buckets of steaming water. Their soles clacked on the wooden grid flooring as they went for more. After dumping the new buckets, the older one said, "You say *winse,* we come chop-chop."

"Fine," he agreed, and when they shuffled off, he undressed and eased himself into the hot water. It felt heavenly as the liquid began soaking into his every pore. He used the bar of soap and washrag, wondering how his partner was faring with her bath.

At last, he was through. "Rinse."

They came clacking along across the grid flooring— each of them with a pail.

"You can stand, otherwise do no good," one of them said, climbing on a chair. She doused him good twice, and then the younger one began to dry him.

He thanked them and took the towel from her. He didn't need any Chinese pussy this evening. Business was slow and they were ready to expand their services, he felt sure.

Dried off and dressed, he tipped them each a dime as he went out. They bowed and thanked him.

The barbershop was only two doors away and the lamp was on inside. The only man in there jumped out of the chair and put away the newspaper. A lean, short man with a sporty mustache, he began talking nonstop as soon as he put the sheet over Slocum. He covered everything from politics in Santa Fe to politics in Washington. The halt in building the railroad due to hard financial times, the economic effects on his business, and how, when the tracks were completed to the West Coast, Lordsburg would be the next economic center of the universe.

Shaved, Slocum paid the man, and hoped he wouldn't be disappointed if Wall Street didn't move there right off. On the walk back in the night to the hotel, he passed several noisy saloons with raucous drunken whores inside raising Cain with customers. A tinny piano or an accordion's music companioned the hell-raising.

In crossing the lobby, he nodded to the clerk, who said, "Your wife's bath was taken care of."

"Very good, sir."

Upstairs, he inserted his key and unlatched the door. The room was dark except for some light coming in the window. She rose and came toward him totally naked. The dim light reflected off her narrow shoulders and pointed teacup-sized breasts.

He tossed his hat aside and took her in his arms to kiss her. "It's dark in here."

"I-I didn't want you disappointed—in me."

He swept her up. "Why would I be?"

"There's not very much of me. Most men like more buxom women."

He kissed her and then raised his face to say, "I like women period and you are lovely."

Her arms flew around his neck. "I'm glad I made such a choice on my first affair."

At the bed, still holding her, he toed off his boots. Then, he set her down gently to undress. "Was the bath hot?" he asked.

"Lovely. I must have washed away a ton of dust." She swept back the covers, and then she rose on her knees to undo his pants while he shoved down his suspenders. His pants fell to his knees and he shed them quickly. When he stood up again, she pulled him toward her.

She took his enlarging dick in her small hand and shook her head, tossing her curly shoulder length hair. "He's big."

"Does that worry you?"

With a mischievous smile, she looked up and shook her head. Then she began to lick the ring of its head and popped the end in her hot mouth. The surface rubbed on the roof of her oral cavity and began to stiffen. Her lips closed around it, and her tongue lashed the shaft until he stood on his toes in wild anticipation.

She backed off and started down backwards, pulling him after her. He settled on his knees and watched her thin legs separate for his entry. As he eased his way between them, she took charge of his stiff column and inserted him in the wet lips of her cunt. With a gentle probe, his dick soon bumped against a tight ring, and she sucked in her breath in obvious anticipation of pain. With care, he worked against it until it began to widen, and then, with steady pressure, he pushed through her loop.

Her hands gripped his braced arms, and she raised her butt off the bed to accept him. "Oh, dear God—" she cried out. "Don't stop. I love it!"

So he began pumping his tight-fitting piston in her cavity. Her hardened clit began to scratch the top of his erection like a claw, and she tossed her head on the pillow in wild abandon. Mouth open, she slung her head back and forth and moaned as their passion heightened. Higher and higher, until she cried out and he felt the rush of her hot juices flowing out around his dick and over his scrotum. She fainted.

Drunk from her wild abandon, she felt limp to him when he rolled her over and put her up on her knees. He reached around and reinserted his dick in her wet slot. Bent over her, he began pushing it into her, gently squeezing her small breasts until she was wide awake.

"Oh, my God," she said as her walls began to contract around his swollen tool. Then, he shoved it to her and blew a shotgun blast of his cum into her.

They both collapsed in a pile. Dazzled and spent, she lay in a ball with her small firm butt against him. Weakly, she reached back and clapped his leg. "Put him back in me. I like him in there."

He obeyed her.

"If poor Hubert was half that big, I'd—I'd sure get a lot more out of life. He only has five inches and it's never very hard."

"Maybe it will grow while you're gone."

She giggled, squirming toward him and inserting more of his dick inside her. "No chance. I've tried it all."

"Good night, Mrs. Culmeyer."

"Good night, Slocum. What a night. Wow."

He agreed. He didn't relish the days ahead searching for Ojo Nevado in the Madres. No way they'd compare to his night with this woman.

Then he wondered if Mrs. Ramsey was even still alive.

5

They were on the move again. Vanessa rode a thin paint pony he'd brought for her to ride so they could utilize her stouter horse as their pack animal. The walls of the towering sheer-faced canyon were less than fifty feet apart. They raced up the sandy dry wash that she knew must rage with floods when heavy rains fell in the mountains above them. It was hot as an oven in the confines, and both her mount and her armpits perspired profusely. The paint's dead-looking uncurried hair was dripping.

She could tell by the tight lines in Snow Eye's face that he was anxious every time he turned in the saddle and looked to their back trail. His words to her had been—*the federales are coming*. Then he'd loaded her and her things quickly and they'd fled their last camp at a spring.

For the first time in their many close brushes with the Mexican military, she felt concerned about their safety. Anxiety at the thought of being captured, and at the notion of being violently raped by the soldiers, upset her stomach. The skin crawled on the back of her neck. Her throat felt so constricted, it was hard for her to get enough air.

He reined up his lathered sorrel horse, waving her to go

on past him. Then he fell in behind her paint and the packhorse, lashing both of them with his quirt. Her horse's sud-
den lurch ahead about unseated her, but she managed to
gain her balance and bent over the saddle horn to urge him
on more.

"Take the trail," Snow Eye shouted, pointing to the side.

On her right, she could see the narrow ledge cut in the
towering bank. It hardly looked wide enough for a horse,
and it spiraled skyward. Her mount slowed up when she
turned him. Then he tripped and fell to his knees, throwing
her forward on his neck. The gelding scrambled to his feet,
and she recovered and pulled him up. To her relief, he felt
sound as he started over more loose rocks and climbed like
the devil was on his heels. The packhorse was loose, but
coming behind on her paint's heels.

"I lost the lead," she shouted back at Snow Eye, realizing how fast they were ascending the mountainside and how
far beneath her the earth was. A great harpy eagle screamed
at her, floating on the updrafts, and added to the fear grip-
ping her.

She forced her focus toward the red sandstone wall
scraping her right moccasin and the blue azure sky above.
Muscles in her legs cramped and trembled. The cooler wind
swept her sweaty face, and she wondered how high they
must go to reach the top.

Dear God, help . . .

Slocum and Naco rode out of Lordsburg in the predawn.
Mrs. Culmeyer stood back in the shadows with her collar
turned up, wrapped tight in her black coat. She nodded
good-bye. He gave her a wave sideways with his right hand
and jogged the new horse on. Perhaps someday, the thin
lady wound tight in a long coat would cross his trail again.
He looked over at Naco and the pack mule, then nodded.
They were off for Mexico on a mining or ranching expedi-
tion.

They crossed the border in the late afternoon, which hardly changed a thing, except that they were in Sonora and no longer enjoyed the protection of U.S. laws and rights. The first village they found was called Verde, but in the slanting bloody light of sundown, there was little green about it. Several horses crowded a hitch rail at a cantina. They looked like American mounts and saddles, rather than the typical vaquero outfits. Slocum made a note of the fact when he dismounted.

"Those horses may be from across the border," he said to Naco when he rode in close. "I better have a look inside first. Stay out here for a moment."

Naco agreed, remaining in his saddle. Slocum pushed his felt hat up with his thumb, reset the .44 on his hip, and elbowed his way through the batwing doors. Several hard faces turned to observe him through the veil of smoke. Even the *putas* grew silent from their places on men's laps where their breasts were being felt up or their crotches being probed with middle fingers.

"Well, look here, guys," a sharp-featured man dressed in black leather said, removing his arm from around the neck of a girl he'd been feeling up and beginning to size up Slocum.

Slocum shook his head. "I come in here minding my own business. I'm looking for some food."

"Oh, Jorge has food. Ain't you, Jorge?"

"Ah, *sí, señor,*" the short balding man behind the bar said.

"Good, fix me two plates." Slocum never took his eyes off the man in the leather clothing.

"Don't I know you from somewhere?" the man said, coming closer.

"I've probably been there."

The man clutched his right elbow in his left hand and used his finger to tap his mouth. "San Juan Arroyo."

"What about it?"

"You shot Curly Rankin."

"He must have had it coming." Who was this bastard after anyway?

"Curly was working for Old Man Ames and you were working for some woman—"

"Mrs. Dyert."

"Yeah, I remember she had great tits. My name's McCory."

"Slocum's mine."

"That was who you were." McCory nodded and folded his arms. "Men said that Curly was as fast as they got with a gun."

"You know, McCory, when you go to believing stuff like that is when a faster man will come along and blow you away."

"Maybe. You needing work?"

Slocum shook his head. "Who's offering?"

"Ike Clanton. See, me and the boys been having us a heyday down here working for the old man. Been making over three hundred a month apiece."

"Sounds like good work."

"Yeah, we've been liberating cattle from the Mex down here. Old man's got him several contracts with the army and Indian agencies for beef. Got us two gold shipments, too. That was gravy. You could make some real bucks with his outfit."

"Here is your food, Señor."

"How much do I owe you?"

McCory waved him away. "I'm buying."

"No, I'm not taking your job and I'd hate for you to waste your money on me."

"I said I was buying." He slapped his hand on the bar. Jorge drew away from the food and retreated against the back bar.

Slocum felt his own face grow cold and his gun hand loose as he worked his fingers to limber them. "This ain't worth fighting over, neighbor."

A small sly smile crossed McCory's thin lips. "I think it is. I don't think you're as fast as they say you are—"

Then the loud click of a rifle being cocked, and the whole place went dead silent. On his belly lying underneath the batwing doors, Naco pointed the muzzle of his .44/40 Winchester at the man.

"Me and Naco are sure hungry. Don't no one come out those front doors for thirty minutes while we eat this food. Everyone savvy that?"

Heads bobbed all over in agreement. Satisfied, Slocum paid Jorge a half-dollar, took the two plates heaped with food, and stepped over Naco to get outside. "I think they understand now."

Naco drew back, and they eased across the street to sit their plates of food on a low adobe wall where they could view the front door and eat their meal.

"What do you think?" the Apache asked, looking suspiciously at the cantina and picking up a burrito to eat under the stars.

"I think he was the buddy of a man I shot in a range war up in New Mexico a few years ago."

"I figured if you gunned him down we'd have to leave real fast, and I was hungry."

"Good thinking. He offered me a job for three hundred a month rustling cattle for Ike Clanton."

"High pay, huh?"

"High enough, except I don't like Ike Clanton."

Naco nodded and tossed his head at the cantina. "They are being awfully quiet in there."

Slocum stopped eating his burrito and swallowed hard, wishing for something to wash down the spicy beans and meat. "Watch the roof. They may send a shooter up there."

Naco nodded and started in on his second burrito. Then he filled his mouth quickly and grabbed up the rifle, all in a flying movement, moments before the man's silhouette appeared on the front edge. The rifle's muzzle fired a red blast, and the boom hurt Slocum's ears. Hard hit by the bullet, the man slumped over the edge and crashed to the ground in a cloud of dust, his spurs ringing.

Slocum chewed slowly on his mouthful before he asked, "You reckon any more in there want to die?"

Naco shrugged, set the rifle down, and went back to eating another burrito.

No one came out to see about the dead man.

They finished eating, and Slocum wiped his mouth on a kerchief from his pocket. "Go over there and slice all those reins. I'll bring the pack mule and your horse. We'll herd them horses out of here ahead of us. That'll stop them from trailing us."

"Good idea."

Like a thief in the night, the bent-over Apache ran full out to the hitch rail, and soon, with their reins slashed loose, the horses flew backward. Slocum on his bay herded them away from the cantina. Naco vaulted into his own saddle from the right, and that shied his new horse into colliding with the pack mule, but they were rolling up the street by then.

"Good job!" Slocum shouted at him.

Yipping like a coyote, Naco set in to waving his coiled-up reata at the horses, and they fled. Behind the herd of galloping saddle horses, with Slocum leading the honking mule, they left Verde. He could still hear those outlaws cussing them out from the edge of town.

He looked back with a smile. Something else to piss Old Man Clanton off. They were off for the Madres to find Snow Eye and Mrs. Ramsey.

6

Mrs. Ramsey tasted sand in her mouth, and some grains stung her eyes. She tried to blink away the grit under her eyelids. Her sweaty finger was curled around the trigger on the new-smelling rifle. A shot from one of the *federales'* rifles had struck six inches from where she lay on her upset stomach under some pine trees. It scared her enough that she drew back.

Then, a shower of pine bark rained down on her from another wild shot at the tree beside her. Thank God the *federales* weren't good shots. Snow Eye had said they were only a patrol and there weren't many. She hoped her lover could count.

Another incoming round from a *federale* Mauser to her right sent dust into the air—no problem. That one wasn't close. She put the rifle to her shoulder and rose up on her knees, ready to shoot. She saw one of the *federales* running at her, and drew a bead on his chest. The blast of gun smoke blinded her, but she saw, for an instant, the soldier throw his arms up in the air and fly backward. She'd killed a man.

She'd shot game before: several deer, two mountain lions who had gotten at her goats, and even several coyotes that ventured too close to her chickens, sheep, and goats. But never a man. Would more try to rush her? Woodenly, she chambered another cartridge in the lever-action rifle.

Then she heard several shots and men yelling for help. They were running in all directions. She took aim at one of them in a green uniform. With the center of his back in the iron sights, she fired. He stumbled forward and fell face-down.

This time, she wasted no time levering in a new round and spun around looking for another target. Her man rode past where the *federale* had fallen in the pines on his new bald-faced horse. He carried a smoking pistol in his right hand. His broad brown bare chest glistened in the shafts of sunlight.

She gathered her skirt and carried the rifle in her other hand as she went to join him.

"The enemy is dead." He jumped off his horse, sticking the revolver in his belt. He grabbed her around the waist and though his gun gouged her, she thrilled at him spinning her around in his celebration.

With her arm wrapped around his head, she kissed him all over his face. "I was afraid. I was so afraid."

He held her out to look in her face, his powerful arm locked under her butt and holding her high. "You killed several of them."

"I know it was us or them."

"You are a great woman. I will never forget this day. I have fought beside strong men who would never have done this. I thank the spirits who sent you to me."

Then she knew that with all this excitement, he would need her as a woman. When he hungrily buried his face in the V between her breasts, thrills rose inside her. Quickly, she undid the blouse for him to graze on them. My God— what a lover, and danger like this always brought out such wild abandon in both of them. Their passion was form- ing wild desire for each other's body. Oh, she craved for

him to be inside her; it was the only thing that ever put out
the fire between her legs.

"Oh, my lover, smother me . . ."

The sleepy-looking village under the palms was called Antioch, named after a place in the Bible. Slocum, Naco, and
the pack mule came up the dusty main street and spooked
off two nervous yellow cur bitches. The third dog, a male,
stopped to bark at the men. Then he must have decided that
the bitches were in heat and were more important than
challenging the new arrivals.

A big man stood in the doorless cantina, his hand holding on to the hand-carved lintel over his head. *"Buenas
tardes, mis amigos.* Welcome to Antioch. I am so glad you
came to see me. My name is Benito. This is my place."

Slocum reined up. "What, Benito, would you have that
we would need?"

"I have some good mescal or some pulque." He held up
two fingers. "I have a young *cabrito* on the fire cooking
right now." His third finger came next. "I have some lovely
putas that would love you all night long."

"What would all this cost us?"

"Oh, *mis amigos*, I could do it all for—five pesos."

"Three."

"Madre Dios. Three pesos? Why, I would go broke in no
time." He slapped his forehead. *"Cuatro pesos*, huh, hombres?"

Slocum tossed his head at Naco. "My man wants to see
the *putas* first."

"Nina, get Anita and get out here quick. We have big
rich customers come to see you girls."

They came out, blinded by the sundown, and tried to see
these rich men. Anita looked potbellied and the other one
was thin, but they weren't old hags.

"Three-fifty," Slocum said, and dismounted.

"You rich *americanos* will be the ruin of me," said Benito.
"All right. What you want first? The women or the goat?"

Slocum tied his horse at the rack and put his arm around Anita's shoulder. "We better eat first, hadn't we, girls?"

"Ah, *sí*, I can eat first, Señor." Her arm shot around his waist and she hugged herself against him as they went inside. "Maybe you could stay a few days, no?"

"We'll see," he said, noticing that Naco had his woman in tow.

"You ever hear of a one-eyed Apache called Ojo Nevado?" Slocum asked Benito, who was setting up the mescal bottle and some glasses.

"*Sí, señor.* You need him?"

"Can you find him?"

The bartender shrugged. "There is a man here who could find him."

"Who is he?"

"A fortune-teller."

"You think he could tell me where he's at?" Slocum looked hard at the man for an answer.

"Ask these women. He is a good man at this business, huh, girls?"

Anita, busy fussing with Slocum's shirt, wrinkled her thick nose and agreed. "Juan could find a missing cockroach."

"Send for him," Slocum said. A good psychic might help him.

The young goat cooked over mesquite wood was mouthwatering. The fresh tortillas the old woman made were excellent, and her frijoles spicy enough that Slocum's breath could have wilted roadside daisies. They were being waited on by the two younger women, who refilled their cups with hot tea. The entire village was out of coffee, they told Slocum. The two women ate hearty as well. The young goat soon became the bones tossed to the cur dogs outside.

The gray-headed man named Juan came too late for any of the goat, but he sat down and ate some frijoles wrapped in corn tortillas.

"Who do you wish to find?" he finally asked them.

"Ojo Nevado—he's an Apache medicine man. He kidnapped a white woman about a week ago, and they said he was headed for the Sierra Madres."

"There are many mountains in this range."

"I know. That's why I am asking you where my friend and I should look for them."

Juan, sitting cross-legged, dropped his chin on his chest as if he was going off into a trance. Anita, standing on her knees, held Slocum's arm against her. "He once told a man when he'd die. The very day he said, a rattlesnake bit the man, and he died before midnight on that day."

"I'm not interested in that," Slocum said. She pushed her breast into his upper arm and smirked at him—like she wanted to do other things, but was waiting for the fortuneteller to say something.

At last, the old man raised his head and nodded. "I saw him beside a rushing river. It is not too wide so it is high up. There is a needle to the east. He has a white woman with him."

"She's all right?" Slocum asked.

"She was fine—they were making love."

Slocum winked at Naco. "You know the country of the needle?"

"It's far up."

"We ain't got anything else to do. *Gracias*, Juan. Can I pay you?"

The man shook his head. "I need no money. People feed me."

"Gracias."

When the man was gone, Slocum paid Benito five dollars for his care. Anita by then had begun to act very impatient with him, and dragged him out of the cantina to a hammock hung between some trees.

"Get undressed," she hissed at him, shedding her blouse over her head and then undoing her skirt ties to step out of it. Standing naked in the leaf-filtered starlight, she raised her arms over her head and stretched on her toes. She did have a small potbelly. She climbed on the bed and sat in the bottom depression hugging her legs—waiting.

"Who are you?" she asked. "Are you a Ranger?"

"No. Do you know a Ranger?"

"I met some in Texas when I was a girl."

"Oh?"

"They were always nice to me."

"How nice?"

"Oh, they were just nice."

She spread her raised knees apart, and he crawled across the spongy net, his every move about to buck her off it. When he stopped at her feet, she raised up and pulled on his erection.

"Oh, he is a *muy grande* prick."

He scooted closer. She eased her butt toward him and they connected. Then she threw her legs straight up so they were beside her face. "Poke it all to me. I'm a big girl."

"Your way." He laughed and pumped all he could inside her.

When he struck her wall deep inside, she cried out, "That's enough, hombre. Oh, you feel so good and he's getting bigger."

She shut her eyes and tossed her head. Braced on top of her legs, he could fondle her sagging breasts, which made her giggle out loud and she grew more excited. Soon, her clit stiffened and she became wilder, hunching him with every shove. Then he felt the needles in his butt, and went to the bottom of her well and came hard. They collapsed.

She woke him in the middle of the night, jacking him off while sitting astride his legs, and then sat down on his half-filled erection and rode him like he was a wild horse, bouncing away on the hammock until he came again and she got bucked off. He fell back asleep—that silly woman . . .

He and Naco rode on the next morning. Slocum felt so hungover, he thought he might fall out of the saddle, and all he'd had to drink the night before was one shot of mescal.

Naco acted no better off, and they rode the desert grease-wood all day to reach a spring in the desert called Cabello Wells.

To Slocum, the place looked more like a graveyard. Dead, bleached white trunks of old cottonwoods went for miles down the dry wash. They long ago had lost their leaves, and high winds had broken off large limbs, but they remained. A dead reminder of a time when water nourished their roots and their dollar-sized leaves invited passersby to stop in their shade. Songbirds once used them as havens from the soaring hawk, and nested high in their branches.

Only one spring spilled into a rock-walled and cement-lined basin, and it no longer ran off down the dry creek bed. The padres had built the holding tank with slave Indian labor. Some say an angry Indian woman, forced to work from sunup to sundown and receiving few rations, had committed suicide by hanging herself in a nearby tree. She'd supposedly cursed the springs never to run again.

Naco said he thought an earthquake had interrupted the flow. That was not unusual in this region below the Madres. Several ranchos that had once been well watered had lost their sources of water to the earth's rumbling, and now sat deserted.

The fire from a dead cottonwood never smelled good, nor was it a hot burn. It was like wood that did not wish to blaze, and smoked rather than gave off heat. Slocum fanned the smoke with his hat until his eyes watered. Naco finally rode off, and came back with a large armload of ironwood and mesquite sticks. Once the fire was ignited, the beans began to boil.

They both sat back on the ground and laughed. Bone-tired, they waited a long time for the beans to cook, and still they were not well done. The two men ate them anyhow, and fell asleep in their blankets.

Dawn came, and they rode on across a land of buzzing sidewinders, a few gaunt long-eared jackrabbits, and lizards scurrying about. Greasewood and scrubby patches of pear

cactus were drought-bitten on the edges of the black shriv-
eled pads. A land that took a high toll of man or beast. Here
and there, a dead horse or burro lay. Its long dry skin, still
with hair on it, lay petrified. The heat waves even distorted
a man's vision of the sawtooth mountains in the distance.

The next day, the Sierra Madres appeared. A hazy range,
still far off, that grew taller and wider as the two men drew
closer. Slocum imagined how, when he was in the mountains, the cool winds in the piney woods would sweep his
face. The only thing that kept him awake and in the saddle
in the day's oppressive heat was the promise of a better
place than the hell they'd ridden across.

"What if we find this white woman and she won't come
back?" Naco asked.

Slocum nodded and considered his reply for the scout.
"I have wondered that myself. If she's alive as they say and
with him, she may not want to leave."

"What then?"

"We tell General Crook she must be dead. No white
woman would turn down being rescued."

Naco nodded with a knowing grin. "Not many anyway."

7

The stinking raw deer hide was stretched over the end of the log. On her knees, she used a knife to scrape the fat and pieces of flesh off the hide. The job was hard and tedious. She stopped many times, and with a whetstone resharpened her thin-bladed skinning knife. When bits of dried meat were gone from that part, she was forced to reposition the pelt on the end of the log and work on another area. The stiff odor from the skin burned her nostrils, and her hands were sore from stretching the skin tight over the log.

Days had passed. There was no more sign of the *federales*. Ojo said the soldiers didn't wish to die and they wouldn't venture too deep into the mountains.

She'd also met the chief of the southern branch of the Chiricahuas, the one they called Who.

His hard, glaring, cruel eyes made her shiver. He was angry-faced all the time, and he'd berated Ojo for even bringing her down to Mexico. But her man paid him no heed. Ojo told her to ignore him. He would choose his own wife.

Ojo had gone to a sweat lodge to look for some sign about the future. His two men had not yet returned with the others he'd asked for, and it concerned him that the army might have captured and killed them. As she worked on the hide, she hoped he had found some good news that day in the sweat lodge. When he was happy, he made passionate love to her.

Then a rough hand grasped her shoulder and shook her—

Slocum and Naco had stopped in the foothills at a small village called Pino Alto for the night. They bought some burritos from a vendor woman, and squatted down eating them beside her.

The woman, who called herself Meia, also squatted on her sandals and kept grinning at them. She pulled her dress over her bony knees to hide her treasure as if she was modest and wore no underwear. "You have a bed tonight?"

"We have bedrolls," Slocum said, not interested in her thin body or her whiny voice.

"You can put them down at my casa." Then she giggled.

"Your food is good. We can find a place to sleep all right."

"You don't want company?"

Slocum shook his head and continued to eat his wrap. Not her company anyway.

"If I knew where you could find gold, would you stay at my casa?"

He stopped eating to answer her. "Why tell us where the gold is?"

She scooted toward him and grinned foolishly "'Cause I like your looks."

"Where's the gold at?"

Her fingers closed on his upper arm and she squeezed the muscle, pressing her small breast against it. "First, we have the honeymoon, then I will show you the mine."

"If there isn't any gold, I'll feed you to the turkey buzzards, one piece at a time, cut off of you while you are still alive."

Wide-eyed, she looked shocked at him. "No, no, you will see it is real. I have a very rich gold mine."

"Why don't you work it?" He still didn't fully trust her.

"Put your hand around my waist." She rose up and lifted her arms.

He discovered that she was really skinny, not just her knees. "Okay, but why—"

She put a finger on his mouth. "Those mountains are full of *bandidos*. I couldn't work the mine, and I couldn't trust anyone to work it for me."

"How did you get it?"

"My husband found it."

"What happened to him?"

"He went to work the mine one day and never came home. They killed him."

"Didn't they find the mine?"

"No. When he didn't come home, I went to find him. But I could tell that he never got to the mine. They must have caught him and tortured him—but he told them nothing."

She shook back the coarse black hair from her face. "There was no way he would have told them anything. He was very much like you. *Mucho hombre.*"

"How far must we go to find it?"

"A few days, but it is worth it."

"You have a horse to ride?" Slocum asked her.

"Ah, *sí, señor.*"

"It better not be a hoax, Meia."

She crossed herself on her bony-looking breastplate. Then she again tried to toss the stringy hair back from her face. Her movements did no good, so in the end, she had to part it with her fingers and push it back with her hands. "I swear on the Mother of Jesus. There is gold up there."

"All right."

"Let's go to my *casa*. I have a corral for the horses and plenty of room. I won't have to cook in the street anymore, now I have such *grande* partners for my mine."

"That would do," he said. The mine, even if it wasn't a good one, might make a good excuse to be in the mountains. She stowed her small cooker and told the two men to follow her.

They led their horses and the pack mule up the steep narrow street. The clop of their hooves echoed in the growing twilight. The jackass brayed noisily at another one in the street, and Naco had to jerk on the lead to get him to move. Winding around, they soon came out on a flat hill, and she led them through some junipers until they came to a jacal and some pens. She motioned to the bald-faced yellow horse in the pen.

"That's an expensive horse," Slocum said to her.

She nodded and smiled. "I did not lie to you about my gold mine."

He looked hard at her. "There was no one in this entire village you trusted?"

"Sure, but—" She snapped her fingers beside her face. "Those *bandidos* in the mountains would have cut their throats in a *momento* and stolen my gold. I needed some tough hombres to help me. There is no one in this village that tough."

"We could be *bandidos* ourselves."

She grinned big, showing the space of a missing tooth. "He's an Apache and you are a plenty tough gringo. I am staking my life and my fortune on you."

"You know what too good to be true is?"

"That's me. Can you put up his horse?" she asked Naco.

He made a smug smile and nodded.

She took the reins from Slocum, handed them off to Naco, and shoved Slocum into the jacal. Then, guiding him to her hammock in the shadowy room, she began to undress. With her skirt off, she stopped and looked at him. "What is wrong?"

"I am trying to figure you out." He gave her a frown.

"There is no time for that."

He narrowed his gaze at her. "Do you have the powers of a *bruja*?"

She was taking the blouse off and stopped.

"No," she said with it still covering her head. Then she began to fight it.

Feeling sorry for her, he reached over and helped her get free. Then he tossed the blouse on top of her skirt on the chest. What the hell—

He wound up his gun belt and toed off his boots as she undid the buttons on his shirt. Now that she was undressed, he decided there was even less of her than he had suspected. In seconds, he was shedding his clothes and she was running her palms over him. Naked, with the night air bathing his bare skin, he swept her up against him and kissed her.

She closed her eyes, and her small fingers teased his scrotum and the rising erection. His hands cupped the small hard halves of her ass. Then he stopped—some noise outside the jacal made him move her aside and sweep up his revolver.

She sucked in her breath and faded back into the shadows. Her elbows tucked against her sides, she clutched her teacup breasts and whispered, "Be careful."

He nodded. Sounds of a scramble, and then a clunk like someone hitting a watermelon.

"Naco?" His fingers wrapped hard around the grips of the cocked .44, he stood back from the open window.

"There is only one," said Naco.

"Good. You got him?"

"*Sí.*"

"Tie and gag him. He'll talk in the morning."

Naco grunted he would. Slocum went and put the pistol back in the holster. "He won't bother us. Are there more of them?"

She swallowed hard. "In Mexico, there are only a few men you can trust, and there are lots of the other kind."

She stepped out and hugged him. "I knew they watched me. But I swear on the Virgin Mary—"

"No need swearing on her," he said. "Get in bed. That Apache won't let them get close enough to bother us."

"Good."

She finally shut up with his erection jacked halfway inside her. After that, she began to moan and cry out in a muted voice of pleasure. Her head tossed from side to side and she breathed hard for air as their pleasure grew. Like the hard, twisted, braided handle of a bullwhip, her small body hunched toward him and her skinny legs locked around him. No stranger to the pleasures of sex, she put her all into it and drew lots out of him. When at last he came, she clutched him hard and wrenched a climax out of her own body. They collapsed in a pile and slept.

Before dawn, she got up, went outside, built a fire, and made tea and warmed some frijoles. Then she squatted on the ground and patted out flour tortillas for them. The boy that Naco had caught the night before told them his name was Gordo. Seated on his butt, blindfolded, and with his hands tied behind his back, he trembled when Naco laid his knife blade's edge to his throat.

"Before he cuts your throat, he'll slice open your sack and pull out your gonads and then stuff them in your mouth. Who do you work for?" Slocum asked him in Spanish.

"Felipe, Felipe Obregon."

"Why did he send you to spy on us?"

"I-I don't know."

"Why?"

"He wanted to know your plans."

"And you were to kill us if you could," Slocum added.

"No—no—"

"We are going to notch your ear if you don't tell us the truth."

"Mother of God, I swear—"

Slocum looked over at Naco and nodded that he was satisfied. He turned back to the young outlaw between them. "If you don't quit this bunch of outlaws and get a job—the next time we meet, your mother will be at your funeral. You savvy?"

"*Sí*—oh, *sí, señor.*"

Naco shoved him facedown in the dirt. "Be quiet until we are gone, too."

They joined Meia and sipped the honey-sweetened tea. Soon, they ate her beans wrapped in the fresh, thin, snowy tortillas.

"Better than Naco's," Slocum said, holding his up.

"Much better," the Apache said and laughed. "I didn't have to cook it."

"You eat," Slocum said to her. "You need it, and we don't need you to wait." It was a tradition of the land that women and children ate after the men. Perhaps that was why she was so thin.

They saddled their horses and closed up her jacal. The soft clop of their horses' hooves on the hard-packed ground reverberated off the walls. Their column wound down through the village, passing the herd of the door-to-door goat milk deliveryman. Squatted down behind one of his animals, he filled a small pail for a swarthy-complexioned woman standing in a doorway. The goats avoided the horses in the narrow confines, pressed to the adobe wall. Then they bleated after them over the intrusion and flopped their ears.

A man with a five-burro string loaded with small water barrels took off his hat as the three riders moved past him. Fighting roosters were perched everywhere, waking the village with their loud crowing. The burros joined in the chorus, and their pack mule had the last word in long, deep, rasping hee-haws.

Slocum was grateful that after their night in bed, the woman said very little but acted pleased. Obviously, she understood that men soon tired of a woman's incessant talking. Also, she had convinced them to go to her mine, which apparently was her goal in the first place

Once clear of the village, they followed the well-worn

trail through the junipers and pinyons that clustered the slopes they climbed. That first day in the higher country, the pungent smell of the evergreens was heavy in the air, but the sun would still be a while topping the range before them.

Slocum twisted in the saddle and looked back at the little village. In the long shadows, it looked half hidden, but even in such a small place, the evil of outlaws lurked.

Where were Ojo Nevado and Mrs. Ramsey? Somewhere up there in front of them in the Madres.

8

They lay in between the blankets with him on top of Mrs. Ramsey. Ojo took his time pumping his great erection into her and then out, like he was savoring her pussy.

"Who was this one who threatened you today?"

"The one they call Scar Face," she said as the fire of passion began to boil from inside her.

"What did he say to you?" He shoved his thick erection back in, making chills run up her spine.

"That I was a *puta* and he wanted to fuck me."

With his cock deep inside her, he rose up higher and tossed his head back. His arms bracing him over her, he shook with the tremors of anger. "Did he leave after that?"

"No. He wrestled with me and felt my breasts. He hurt me and I stabbed him in the leg with my small knife. I would have cut his sack open and spilled his *huevos* out, but he saw my anger and ran away."

"Ah. You did good, my white flower." As he dropped down on top of her to go deeper so that their bellies were meshed together, he whispered in her ear, "He will never know how good you are at this."

His great horn ripped her clitoris to life, and she cried out in the arms of pleasure.

"Oh, Ojo, I don't care what he missed. I have you." Her body in a ball to accept all of him, she floated away in the clouds. Later, when he was through with her, it would be another night when she could sleep until near dawn, physically and emotionally drained. Dazzled and breathing so hard her heart pounded, she lifted her hips and hunched harder at him. Onswell was never this good—never.

Slocum and company camped in the pines that evening. Meia made them supper, frying some back strap from a fawn that Naco shot. They couldn't use a large animal carcass without wasting it. Besides, the milk-fed young deer would be tender. Meia said she planned to use the hide to make herself a soft leather purse-bag. While her food cooked, Slocum and Naco scouted north and south for any sign, but they returned to camp from both directions without finding anything useful.

She raised up and pointed her long fork to the south. "I hear a pack train coming."

Naco agreed.

"Wonder who it is," Slocum said, lounging on the pine-needled ground.

"Some packer taking supplies to a mine or packing out rich ore." Naco shrugged and went to see about it in the growing twilight.

"Watch yourself. These are not usually friendly people," Slocum said to him.

Meia agreed with a grim nod. Naco was already gone in the long shadows of the towering pines. Slocum sat up and brushed the needles off his shirtsleeve. "Guess we'll find out who they are soon."

"They must be coming to use the spring," she said, and rose to bring him some more coffee. With a wary look in that direction, she smiled. "We are maybe a day and a half from the mine."

"Good. What if there are high-graders working it?"

She looked at him and pursed her lips. Then she shook her head. "They can't find it. How to get in the mine, I mean."

"Well, someone found it."

"My husband made a new entrance after the original one caved in."

"So all they'd find is a cave-in?"

She nodded quickly and tossed her head at the sound of the mules braying. "Later, can we take our blankets away from them if they camp here?"

"Sure."

"Good," she said, rising and searching the trail coming off the mountains.

He twisted to see what she was looking at. The bloody golden rays of sundown that filtered through the tree trunks shone on a bearded man astride a thick-set roan mule in the lead.

"Know him?" he asked.

"His name is Arturo. He raped me once."

Slocum nodded. "Up here?"

"Yes."

"Ah, Señor," Arturo said in a loud voice as he halted his train. "I see you beat me to the spring. May I water my animals and then we will move on?"

At the sight of her, he swept off his shapeless weathered sombrero. "Ah, Señora Malone, I did not see you at first. How are you today?"

"Very well," she said, standing straight-backed and with a cold glare in her eyes for the man.

"Did you ever find your husband who ran off?"

"No," Slocum said, rising to his feet. "Now she's with me. Water your horses and mules, then move on."

"Most men would invite me to supper." He grasped the big saddle horn in his fist and rocked the mule by swaying back and forth in the saddle.

"You have no welcome here."

He motioned toward her. "Did she tell you I made love to her?"

"She called it rape."

"Ah, hombre—" He held his hands out in surrender. "Love, rape. What is the difference, huh, amigo?"

"Water your stock and ride on. And be quick."

"Come, my *compañeros*." He waved his arm over his head for his riders to bring their horses and mules forward. "There is no friendship here."

He booted his mount, then leaned back, checked Slocum, and took off his hat again for Meia in a sweeping gesture. "Ah, Mrs. Malone. This is *mucho gringo* you have now, huh?"

She never answered him.

"I said water them and be gone. That Apache up there with the .44/40 only needs one word from me and you'll be popping up daisies."

Arturo looked back, but the last glare of the sun was too bright for him to see Naco. He turned around, nodded as if impressed, and spurred his mule after the other three packers with the twelve heavily loaded mules. No doubt they carried high-grade ore in their panniers.

"He's gone," Slocum said, and stepped over to hug her shoulder. He felt her shivering like it was ice cold.

"I am not a *puta*. He forced me down and raped me."

"I'm sorry."

She clung to him. "I was Malone's wife. He married me when I was very young. I knew no other man."

"I believe that."

She spat in the direction Arturo had gone. "That sumbitch caught me in my blankets one night when I was up here looking for my man. He is not a lover, he's a dog, and has a skinny dick like one. I hated him the whole time he was on top of me—he did not last long."

"He's a bully."

A toss of her hair and she wrinkled her small nose. "What does that mean?"

"Someone who picks on the ones weaker than him."

She nodded in agreement and waved to Naco, standing on the high point cradling his rifle. "Our food is ready."

When the Apache joined him, Slocum asked, "You know this Arturo?"

"I think he once raped and killed an Apache girl who was picking berries."

"See," Meia said. "He's a bully."

"We better be careful tonight," said Slocum. "He may want our guns and horses, too."

Naco nodded. "He needs to be watched."

"We can take turns standing guard. He's not a stupid man, but I could see the deep-rooted cruelty in his speech and the way he looks at others."

A quick glance toward her. She agreed with a nod.

They ate their venison, beans, and tortillas in the twilight. With the sun already swallowed far in the west, the dull light that came after twilight settled in and the night animals began to emerge. An owl hooted for its mate, and a coyote did the same in a mournful howl. Then, as if to show off, a red wolf up on the mountain used his loud voice to cut the night in a wailing howl.

"I'll take the first shift," Naco said, and started to leave.

"You know the others?" Slocum asked.

"Just men."

"I think I battered his pride, so he'll be back for another round."

Naco nodded.

She was busy bent over washing their plates in a shallow dishpan, but now she looked up. "You have no home? No woman?"

"This is my home and you are my woman."

"Strange." With her hand, she pushed back the hair from her face. "I would think you owned a large ranch and had many family. You aren't like men I have known who have no roots."

"I have no family, no ranchero."

"Then there is a reason." She went back to her chores.

"I was playing cards one night and a young man lost all his money. He came back later drunk and wanted to kill me. I killed him instead."

"So?"

"His grandfather was a very powerful man and had me accused of murdering him. Of course I rode away. But he keeps two Kansas deputies on my back trail."

"It was self-defense?"

"Not in his eyes, and he is rich and very politically strong where he lives."

"Oh, I am sorry."

"Life treats us all cruelly at times. See, I'd probably never have met you if it hadn't been for him." Slocum chuckled.

She dried her hands and came over to sit in his lap. "That was good, no?"

"Fine for me." His arms hugged her tight.

With her palms, she held his face and kissed him. Then, a smile of approval and a nod followed. "You are a big hombre."

"You're a little one. Come on. It won't be long till my guard duty starts."

She hugged his waist. On their way to the trees, he swept up the bedroll. They'd need that, for the night would cool fast. Arturo and his bunch had ridden on, but Slocum wasn't any more satisfied than Naco that the man wouldn't try something. A man like that didn't take being run off without a grudge. Besides, he wanted some more of her. A few weeks up here by one's self with only a calloused hand to jack off made a man think even about a thin woman.

Meia wasn't bad to make love to, but she wasn't a bedful of flesh, muscles, and boobs. But when a man had vacated his *cojones* of their seed, who cared about beauty or lots of flesh to knead anyway?

Later in the bedroll, when he climbed off her, he listened in the night.

"Hear anything?" she asked, sounding sleepy and snuggling to him.

"Nothing."

She pulled him toward her. "Then we can do it again."

With a shake of his head, he chuckled at her suggestion. "We better catch some sleep. This may be a long night."

Clouds had shrouded the moon. And a fine mist had begun to fall when he left her half asleep under the canvas cover in the warm blankets and shrugged on his slicker.

"I never saw a thing," Naco said as they squatted under the pines.

Slocum held out his palm to test the light falling moisture. "Strange rain. It usually thunders when it rains up here, and that's about always in the daytime. Late afternoon showers."

"This is very fine. No wind either."

"Get some sleep. This moisture may dampen their spirits."

"I hope so."

With a nod, he sent his man off to catch some shut-eye for a few hours. Settling down with his back to a pine tree above the camp, he felt he could see any changes that came, though his vision was reduced by the darkness and the fine falling rain.

Time passed slowly like there were brakes on each hour. He shifted several times, feeling achy from the dampness and cool air as well as from sitting so long in one place. He fought to stay awake, but managed—

Then something struck him and his world went black. He awoke sprawled on the ground, droplets striking his face. He realized they'd snuck up and knocked him out. What about Meia? The dark night felt empty, and his dull mind was pounded by a hard headache. He groped around in his black world. Found his sodden hat and put it on.

His rifle was gone. Somehow, they'd missed his .44. It was still in his holster. He moved to the bedroll—empty. That son of a bitch. Lost in the darkness, he vowed he'd get her back and make Arturo pay for all the pain he caused her.

Where was Naco? He blindly moved around the campsite. How long had he been out? No telling. Then, like a drunk, he stumbled over a body. On his knees, with his thumbnail he struck a gopher match, using his hat brim as a shield to keep it lit. The death mask of the Apache lying on his back shone wet in the match's glare. Slocum sprawled on all fours and beat the ground with his fists, his loud voice hardly penetrating the sound of the falling rain.

"You sons a bitches will pay! Pay! Pay for this!"

He soon discovered they'd taken the horses and mule, too. At the place where they'd been tethered, nothing remained. His head aching enough to make him dizzy, he dropped down and sat on the ground. It would be sunrise before he could start to find them.

What would he do with Naco's body? He couldn't leave him for the buzzards and other scavengers. But without a shovel, his options were few. At last, using the long knife that the dead scout wore, he began the grave. The gravelly ground gave him little assistance, but holding the knife in both hands and plunging it into the dirt and stones, he soon began to loosen the ground and used his hands to scoop out the soil.

Damn them anyway.

9

"Let go of me," she ordered. "Ojo will kill you!"

She felt herself being crushed against the muscular body of the stinking buck who held both her arms in a steel grip. His harsh dark face looked like that of an angry fighter. Why had this one chosen her?

His words in Apache were guttural and she understood none of them, but he shoved her aside like trash and she fell down. The drop to the hard ground hurt her ass, and she rubbed it under the leather skirt while keeping her eye on the vengeful-looking buck.

Ojo appeared and looked at her, then at the intruder. It was as if he had seen the entire altercation, and he now had his large shiny knife drawn.

His challenge was obvious. But she cried out to stop him. "No, he made a mistake. You need every man here. He won't do it again."

Both men stood a few feet apart, staring at each other, knives ready. Would they stay apart, or would she lose her lover in this foreign land and become the whore of this band to survive? *God. Please make him heed my words.*

* * *

The sun was well up when he finished covering Naco's grave with huge boulders so no vermin would dig him up. Slocum's hands were bloody from the abrasive gravel and dirt he'd dug to lay his friend and great scout to rest. Seated on his butt, he considered what he could carry and would need to take with him. He had to put the rest of the food up high enough so no bears or varmints could get into it in case he needed to come back and use it.

Past noontime, he set out on their trail. The skies had cleared and the air warmed with the sunshine. He'd even begun to dry out. He wore a backpack he'd made for the trip. No telling how far he'd have to go to find a horse or something to ride.

The trail bore signs of them going west like he suspected. Many tracks were old, from other mine supply pack trains that brought supplies in where a wagon could not go and, like Arturo, brought high-grade ore out on the return trip. When he finally reached the edge where the pathway hugged the side of the mountain, he could see the dazzling switches back and forth that led to the land far below.

Buzzards rode the updrafts, making lazy circles far below him. His wet boots were at last drying, but his toes still felt soggy. The loose gravel on the single-file trail proved sharp, and he realized that his hand-made footgear would not last long on such terrain. His boots, built by a craftsman in Nogales, were made for use in stirrups, not marching like a foot soldier in the spiny razor-edged mountains of Mexico. Nothing he could do about that but keep going. There was no sign of the pack train on the mountain, so they were already crossing the desert.

His best chance to catch them would be if they paused at some small village and celebrated. If not, he'd find them sooner or later. Poor Meia. Mrs. Ramsey would have to wait, too. After descending several hours, he took a breather and sat on a great rock to view the rest of Mexico beneath him. He removed his hat to wipe his sweaty forehead on his sleeve. All day he'd chided his carelessness, which had allowed them to creep up on him. But for them to take Naco unaware and kill him meant they were damn tough and skilled at that sort of thing.

He missed the Apache's quiet company as much as he missed having a horse to ride. On his feet he strode down the trail, knowing it would be long past dark before he made the base. He planned to camp there, hoping to find a spring to refill his canteens.

The trails in and out of the Madres were like spiderwebs, and this one was new to him despite his many trips into the mountains. With the bloody sundown falling fast, he found a small spring along the way and quenched his thirst besides filling his small canteens. Gnawing on peppery jerky, he decided the three-quarter-moon would be up a few hours after the sundown that fast fled him.

He found a place off the trail behind some boulders so no one would stumble over him on the trail. He closed his eyes and shut out the roaring in his ears left from the blow to his head. Lucky. They must have thought they'd killed him with the blow. Wrapped in the blanket on the hard ground, he wondered how Meia was doing—how bad that damn Arturo was treating her.

Later, when he woke, his eyes troubled him as he tried to focus in the moonlight. Perhaps that blow had done more damage to him than he'd originally thought? No telling. His leg muscles ached, and were slow to loosen up when he started out again. It was no place to be clumsy. Hundreds of feet to his left was open air, a fall that a man could not survive without wings. He sure had no wings or ability to float in the thin atmosphere.

At dawn, he reached the base. His head pounded like a spike someone was driving into a railroad tie. He drank some water from his canteen and chewed on jerky, but kept walking. The junipers soon gave out in favor of greasewood and cactus. Dry bunchgrass grew shorter and the pear beds sprawled out like fairy rings. Every little while he stopped, wiped his sweaty brow, and let his hair air out in the growing sun's heat. Aside from their tracks and horse apples in the dust, he had no company besides a few lazy rattlesnakes shaking their jointed tails from the security of some shade, and several desert wrens flitting around that scolded him in shrill tunes.

The day dragged on one footstep after another. His headache grew worse. Nothing helped it. He even stopped for a short while and squatted in the shade of a dry wash bank to escape the sun's penetrating rays. No relief came to him, so he pushed on.

Damn. A mirage of water reflected ahead of him. He shook his head while his dry mouth urged him to dive into the clear blue water—anything to clear his pounding head and the dizziness that threatened to swarm him in waves that matched the heat waves that distorted his vision of the land ahead.

At once, he began to stagger—the too-bright world tilted. On his knees, he painfully tried to keep moving. But that, too, like the sun, went out. Last thing he recalled was the taste of the alkali dust.

He awoke on a blanket that moved slow and bumpy. Then he saw an angel—*was this heaven?* How had he gotten here?

"Señor," she said in Spanish. "Close your eyes. The sun is too bright. You are very sick and I am taking you to my grandmother who is a doctor."

"Sick? I . . . need to . . . you . . . don't . . ." Then he passed out again, unable to muster enough strength to even protest.

It was nighttime when he awoke. There must be a ceiling over him because he could not see the stars. Then he noted the sticks and the palm fronds piled on the rafters. It was a ramada. Where was the angel he saw, or was she a dream, too? Why was he seeing everything double?

"Don't try to get up," the authoritative voice of a woman said.

In the small fire's red yellow light, he could see two faces that were wrinkled as dried apples. "Where am I?"

"This place has no name."

"You either?"

She cackled. "You still have some humor. They call me Grandmother."

He nodded with his head on the pillow, which was stuffed with something stiff. "Grandmother, my name is Slocum."

"What happened to your horse? He die?"

"How did you know I even had a horse?"

"Those boots you wear weren't made for walking." She nodded toward them.

"They stole my animals, killed my friend, and took a woman."

"Mean bastards. I guess they thought they'd killed you?"

"Yes, ma'am."

"You have a bad bruise on the side of your head. I would say from a rifle butt. An ordinary man would never have gotten up again."

"My head sure does pound."

"I have some medicine tea you could take. You would call it willow tea. It would help. But you need something stronger now so you can sleep and heal."

"They are getting miles farther away."

She looked at him, exasperated. "Without your strength, how far could you go?"

He nodded. "Will that cure me?"

"Time." Hands locked behind her gray head, she rocked back and forth, sitting cross-legged and nodding in agreement. "Time and rest will heal you."

"Those killers—" He blinked his eyes, hoping the double vision would go away.

"They will be there when you are stronger."

Over the next few days, his vision was no better and he never saw the "angel" who brought him there. Grandmother put many compresses on his forehead. Some smelled bad, but laudanum cut his headaches and put him to sleep.

One evening, as she knelt beside him, she put her small hand on his forehead and went into a trance. He was so tired of the pain and bad vision that he had begun to wonder if he ever would get better. His entire body had begun to stiffen against forces driving him half crazy with the hurting inside his skull.

"I have sent for a witch doctor," she said at last. "I am sorry that I did not send for him sooner, but I thought I could heal you."

"Is he good?"

"The best."

Slocum nodded. Might as well. He was lying flat on his back, unable to fight off an attack. And his gray, fuzzy double vision was no better. He was in a place with no name and a grandmother for a doctor—and she had sent for some other fake doctor to help her. Damn, it might have been better if Arturo had killed him. He was no value to Meia in her time of need, or Mrs. Ramsey. If she even needed him. Damn.

The witch doctor came the next day. A stoop-shouldered, quiet man who sat cross-legged on the ground and talked to him for what Slocum considered hours. How was this? How was that?

At last, he spoke to Slocum and Grandma. "We must bind his eyes so they get no light for seven days. Resting them from having to focus on any light might bring them back with better vision."

Slocum agreed. He'd do anything to have his vision back.

"Your brain needs to rest and heal, too. I have medicine for you that might give you some dreams, but you will rest and not feel anxious."

Anxious, that was the word to describe how he felt all the time. "What do I owe you?"

"Only to get well. She has done good things for you. Maybe this will work better."

So she bound his eyes, and then she gave him the potion

in a tea. In a short while, he slipped into a trance in his own cavern of darkness, and he felt like he was floating. They undressed him and rolled him on his stomach. He could feel the hot wind on his bare skin, and they began to rub him down with a strong-smelling liniment. Must have been several women—they talked in low voices, and when they rolled him over and discovered his partial erection, they giggled, but never quit rubbing him down. Small, powerful, calloused hands were kneading in the pungent lotion.

He could only guess at what they looked like, or what they thought of his flagstaff, but they talked about it.

"He's too big for you," one teased.

"Shush. We don't know if he's asleep or not."

"I'd still like to try him."

"They would have to put stitches in your snatch if you ever tried to stuff that big cock in you."

"Should we jack him off?" Then the one who spoke giggled.

"No."

He felt her take it by the root to steady it, and soon her tongue began to work up the shaft. Hot and like sandpaper, her attention grew more serious. The others must have sat back to watch her—they'd stopped rubbing him and made oohs and aahs as she continued her oral attack. He dared not move a muscle—it would scare them away—but the ballooned head of his dick wanted to move deeper.

She slapped the shaft to arouse it, then moved in again with her mouth. At last, he knew she better be ready and he came. The others applauded when she raised up. He could imagine the white streams flowing from both sides of her mouth and running down her chin. He decided she'd taken a real load, and the others around her sounded awed talking about her bravery.

"Maybe sometime when he's awake I can finish this?"

"I'd love to watch. He's all rock-hard muscles."

"Rosa, maybe we can all watch you take him on."

"Hush, Grandmother is coming back."

They went back to work on him, rubbing and massaging in the lotion that relaxed him as much as the medicine the man had left him. If only he'd be able to see when the week was over—the things they gave him and the time had helped. His head didn't pound like it had before. This made him feel better, too.

He dropped off to sleep, and began to dream about Rosa and him making love.

10

Their battle would be to the death. Ojo's woman had been offended. The one called Wolf Eyes had stepped over the line, mauling her like she was some kind of *puta*.

Ojo stepped in and slashed the man's forearm above his knife hand. The worst place for Wolf Eyes to take a cut. He shifted his large knife to the other hand, but he did not look as certain with the weapon as when he'd had it in his right hand. Red blood dripped off his right fingertips.

"Why did you bother her?" Ojo asked.

"She is just a white woman. A *puta*. Why do you defend her?"

"She is my woman!" Ojo leaped at the buck with all his fury. He slashed his neck, and then slammed his own chest into Wolf Eyes. Fending off the man's left arm and crowding him, Ojo drove the knife in his back to the hilt.

Wolf gurgled his last breath. His knees buckled and he folded into a pile. Then, as his life evaporated, Ojo wrenched his knife from his back. With a quick look around to see if there was anyone else to challenge him or his woman, he wiped the blood off the blade on his loincloth and nodded to her.

"I am sorry this one bothered you. They will learn you are my woman."

Shocked by the brutality of the whole thing, she swallowed and nodded. Being an Apache's wife was harder than being a polygamous wife. But it had its rewards, and she would get hers later that night in the blankets.

Despite the hot sun, she shuddered in revulsion. This was a much tougher world than she had ever known or even realized.

"If we kill each other," another Indian squatting in the group under the shade of small mesquite said, "we will have none to fight the white eyes."

"They must honor the ways of the people. Would he have done that to a Mexican woman I took as my bride?" He searched around, looking hard at all of them. "No, but she is white. Our worst enemy for years had been the Mexicans. So why would she be so special?"

They gave him no reply.

"Leave her alone and guard her for me when I am gone. Hear me?" His sharp brows hooded, he searched their faces for reactions.

The other solemn-faced Apaches agreed.

In approval, she nodded at him. If others saw or heard about this, they'd leave camp if they didn't like it, but no one was fool enough to challenge him. Her man was chief, and more young men were coming in one or two at a time to join his band.

As she grew excited, she also dreaded the thought of him taking on the Mexican soldiers. But Ojo even knew how they thought—they'd rather have been in bed with a *puta* than fighting him and his men. And given half a chance, they'd run back to the *puta* for more.

A world without light had made Slocum's ears have keener hearing. He lounged in the hammock. Grandmother came out in the backyard. "You are better?"

"I can't see beyond this mask."

"Good, then your eyes are resting."

"Whatever you say. This outlaw Arturo that has Meia. Do you hear anything about him?"

"No, but I don't hear about everything."

"Look in your looking glass and tell me if you can see them."

"How do you know I even have one to look into?"

"My ears are not plugged. They work well."

"So you have been listening?"

"What am I supposed to do? Lie here and act bored?"

"I will look tonight, but don't expect good news."

"I won't." He wanted to know, and his confinement to the hammock only added to his frustration about not being able to help Meia.

Rosa brought him food and told him his burritos were hot. She had some red wine for him, which he'd given Grandmother money to buy. She had no wine herself and he knew, even in his dark world, that she had no money. Even poor Mexicans had money for red wine.

"We will be sad to see you leave us," Rosa said with her usual happy-sounding voice. "We have little income to buy food and wine, of course, and you have been providing for all of us."

"No problem. You all have taken good care of me. Tell me about Rosa," he said between bites of the rich-tasting beans and meat.

"Oh, I am nobody. I was born in a little village in the desert. When I was fourteen and the oldest of seven kids, my father traded me for two burros that would work. He always wanted a team and he hated oxen. These were matched burros and very hard workers."

"Who did he trade you to?"

"A German named Herman who was a trader passing by. He had a string of pack burros that he carried trade goods on. He sold mirrors, beads, needles, such things to women. You know the kind of man, with a bushy black beard and hair all over his body.

"I saw all that hair in the dark that night with him. I thought, oh, Rosa, a great bear is going to rape you the first time."

"Did he?"

"Did he? Why do you think he gave my father those two good burros, because I was good-looking and he needed company? No, because he wanted some young pussy."

"And he got some?"

"Morning, at noon, and at night again. I was too sore to walk. Either my hole down there was good, or he was really starved for it. But I soon learned how to excite him before he got his cock stuck in me, and then once he was inside of me, he would come real quick. He didn't care as long as his balls shot off."

"So how long did you live with Herman?"

"A few months. He got drunk one night and passed out. I took a little of his money and his best riding animal and snuck off. I thought I was far enough away, but he hired some hombre called Santos Bigato. He caught me taking a bath in a small river about sundown one evening, and ran me down with his horse in the water. He caught me by the hair and drug me to the shore—he was so mad, he threw me on the ground and raped my ass.

"That hurt worse than anything ever happened to me. Oh, it was so humiliating, too. Here I am facedown in the dry grass and stickers and he is poking a pecker big as a horse up my butt hole."

He nodded that he understood her, then lifted his mug and finished his wine. "He took you back to Herman?"

"Yes. I have more wine," she offered, and he handed her the cup. "Yes, he took me back to Herman, who kept me tied up until we got to Ansel. You ever been to Ansel?"

He shook his head.

"There is a gold mine there and lots of men are there without women. They all must have a hard-on. He charged a peso a round for me. After six or seven a night of them climbing on me, I quit counting.

"Soon as they came, he'd jerk them off me and he had another waiting to stick it in me. After the business was done, he tied me up and left me there in camp while he went off and got drunk. There was a boy by the name of Janos who liked me, and he found out what Herman did after hours. And when Herman was gone to get drunk, he came by to talk to me.

"He promised to take me away. I said it was too dangerous, but I wanted to get out of there, too. So I gave him a blow job that night to clinch the deal, and we kept an eye out for a good chance. He liked that, and I knew he'd be loyal to me.

"A week later, he had supplies, two good horses, and a pistol." She was on her knees beside Slocum. "We rode all that night and the next day. We stayed on guard night and day when we stopped. I had my first lover and I loved him." She undid Slocum's pants, and then rose up in the hammock to force the suspenders off his shoulders.

In seconds, she had his britches worked down to his knees. "You won't get more blind from me doing this to you?"

"No." He ran his fingers through her thick hair.

"Good. I been wanting to do that with you again."

"Again?"

"You knew, when I did it last time to you." They both laughed.

"What happened to you and that boy?"

He felt her nod her head against the front of his bare legs.

"Santos caught us in the foothills. He stabbed Janos with a knife. I ran over and got Santos's pistol out of his holster from behind. I didn't know you had to cock it. Janos shouted, 'Pull the hammer back.' I did and shot Santos in the ass. The gun smoke burned my eyes.

"I shot him too late. He had already cut Janos's throat because I had been so slow shooting him. I saw my lover lying on the ground, and I was blind mad, and I went to emptying the pistol in Santos's body. After that, I came here and moved in with Grandmother. The other girls here have sad stories, too."

He felt her lift his half-erect dick and kiss the nose. He couldn't escape her. One small hand cradled his balls, and the other hand encircled the base of his rod. Soon, her hot mouth and tongue attacked him. She was wilder than a dust devil tearing across a desert flat, and her enthusiasm for her work swept him away when she tried to swallow the whole thing.

The torment went on and on. Her trying to tear the end off his rigid skintight shaft, and him clutching her thick hair to keep her at work as he grew dizzier by the second with the excitement. Then, he knew the world would explode and arched his back toward her.

She only went harder and faster until he exploded in her mouth, and then he came a second time. With her arms wrapped around his legs to steady herself, she cried.

"Oh, I'm so sorry." She sobbed. "But I needed that."

"Here," he said, collapsing back on the hammock. "Lie with me and I'll hold you."

"I can't," she whispered.

"Why not?"

"'Cause I'd be riding your pole in a few minutes."

"What would that hurt?"

"Do you know what a nymphomaniac is?"

"Yes, I do."

"I think I am one of them. Oh, my pussy itches for it."

"So?" He hugged her to his chest. She was a nicely built young woman and he could feel it as she clung to him.

"You asked for it," she said, and he could hear her undressing while using him for her balance. "You may never see again when I get through with you—no, not really. I want you to see."

"Let's try that then."

"Me making you blind?"

"Sure." He felt her sweep her thick hair back and then guide herself slowly down on his shaft. It would be a long night. A real long one.

11

The sound of shots woke Mrs. Ramsey in the darkness.

Ojo laid a hand on her shoulder. "Take my medicine bag and the good Navajo blanket. Run up the canyon and get on your horse. Go up the back way. It will be steep, but you must cross it before sunup. Keep moving. I will find you. Never fear."

"Yes. May God be with you." She quickly fit her moccasins on her feet and did as he said. Blanket slung over her shoulders, the strap of his medicine bag around her neck, she struggled in her long dress up the steep slope and through the junipers.

Looking back downhill in the weak predawn light, she could see the puffs of smoke from guns. Recalling his warning, she went faster. Swallowing hard, she took only her pony. The packhorse complained, and she wished he would shut up. She bellied up and threw her leg over her horse's back, and he started up the steep mountain though the junipers—she'd always called them cedars. Her mount lunged up the face of the hill, and she had to ride it or slide off his tail.

Once or twice, she dared look back, but she saw little of

anything. Still, she could hear the war cries and rattle of gunfire. Soon, the wind swept her face and the first golden spears of sunlight came across the world. At last on top, she booted her horse on as Ojo had told her. "I'll find you." Those words echoed in her ears. Fear—fear that he might be wounded or injured bothered her. It made her stomach roil.

She reined up and then vomited off the side of the horse. The sourness scorched her nostril and she gagged again, but it was dry. Wiping her mouth on the back of her hand, she shook her head. Was she with child? She who had never carried an embryo longer then a few months? No way, she'd never been pregnant for long—she booted the horse on. Maybe, maybe she would have his son. *God grant me that wish.*

Slocum's eyes were so weak when they took off the binding, even inside the dark jacal they hurt, but he was seeing single.

"What do you see?" Grandmother asked.

"I see the four of you—once."

"Good. You better not leave them open for over a few hours," she said. "They must rebuild."

He nodded. He was relieved that his vision was back, or going to be. "I thank you, ladies. Now I need a horse and saddle. Can you buy me one?"

Grandmother nodded. "Rosa will look for one for you. It might take a day or two."

"That would be fine." Rosa was as he thought: short, with the shapely body he recognized from being in the hammock with her naked, and there was a big grin written on her face.

So he stayed in the shade and even put on the binding later in the day as Grandmother had instructed. He was anxious to get on his way, but he knew that to rush the use of his eyesight might cause a setback, and he needed it to track down Arturo. As well as survive as a man on the run.

So he was still trapped in this place, and as he started to take a siesta, he wondered before he fell asleep if he'd ever regain all his faculties so he could leave.

That evening, they had a feast. Slocum bought two fat young kids from a boy who brought them by, and there was a festive mood. Chinese lanterns were hung and everyone took a bath. The women scurried around like desert quail going here and there with their many skirts held up so they didn't trip on the hems.

Amused, he watched them. He felt grateful for the return of his sight so he could see all of the women again. Camila, a short and thicker-built girl, brought him some wine. "Those *cabritos* are very fat. They will be good."

"I can't wait," Slocum said, and took the pottery mug from her with a nod.

She blushed. "Neither can I."

He sipped it slowly. His recovered vision brought him the sight of hips turning and the shaking of their breasts under the thin cloth of blouses that exposed dark nipples like rosettes. Yes, being blind would be a sad thing for a man who appreciated women so much.

They ate sitting in a circle cross-legged on the floor. Sucking on the bones and tossing the bare ones to waiting dogs, which took them and fled, not wishing to share with the others. All of Grandmother's girls were so busy eating that nothing could disturb their fiesta.

"Have you looked in your glass?" Slocum asked the older woman.

"I have. I saw a woman running from the *federales* all by herself on horseback."

"Was she Mexican?"

"No."

"That could be Mrs. Ramsey. Was she in the mountains?"

"I saw juniper trees."

"I see. Nothing else?" he asked.

"I saw a dead woman, but I could not see her face."

Was Meia dead?

"She was Mexican by her dress."

Slocum thanked her, still deep in thought about who the dead woman could be.

"I spoke to a man today," Rosa said. "Who promised me a sound horse and saddle in two days."

"Gracias." In that length of time, he should be seeing well enough to get on the trail of Arturo. He owed that bastard for killing his friend Naco. And poor Mrs. Ramsey being chased by the Mexican army was also a problem. He'd been in messes before, but this one must be the worst— getting Arturo was his number-one goal at the moment. Then somehow get Mrs. Ramsey out of the hands of her latest captors—whoever they were.

That evening, Rosa woke him, slipping in his hammock and pressing her cool smooth skin to his.

"I am yours," she whispered.

Half propped up in the starlight, he nodded at her. My God, it was delightful to see tits shake again. He pushed the hair back from her face and kissed her. This would be more pleasurable than before when he had to feel for everything. Sprawled on her back with him between her legs, she sighed.

"I will hate that bastard when he brings that horse for you."

His half-filled erection slid in her gates as she moved slightly under him, and she threw back her head. "Put out my fire."

And he did.

In the cool predawn, he awoke and went to the far edge of the yard to relieve his bladder. Pissing a silver stream in the dark shadows of the low wall, he heard a dog growl.

Something was wrong. Then two men's low voices. "—that must be her place."

"*Sí*—where is he sleeping?"

Easy as he could, he slipped back barefoot to the hammock and drew his .44 out of the holster, straining to hear the men. Then he quickly pulled on his pants, still listening for them.

"You take the front. I'll take the back way," one said in a stage whisper.

Slocum saw the silhouette of the intruder's sombrero above the wall as he came down to the gate. The man stepped through the gate, looking all around.

"Drop the gun," Slocum ordered in Spanish.

The man whirled with the pistol in his hand. Taking no chances, Slocum aimed and shot the man in the chest. The invader was struck hard, and his pistol made a second shot in the dirt as he crumpled to the ground.

Slocum rushed to the back door of the cabin, and saw the second man's outline in the doorway. The outlaw began to shoot wildly—Slocum aimed and took him out with his first shot.

Grandmother's women began to scream and cry. "He shot Camila!"

Slocum rushed to the outlaw and knelt beside him. "Who are you? Tell me or I'll whack your balls off before you die."

"Manuel—"

"Who do you work for?"

"Ar—turo."

"How did you find me?"

"Francisca—sent him word."

"Who's she?" He turned to the girls working on the wounded girl under a candle lamp.

Rosa brought him a lamp and made an angry face. "The wife of the man who was supposed to bring you a horse and saddle. That bitch."

Then the other girls began to wail across the room. "She's dead. Mother of God, the poor thing is dead."

Slocum held Manuel by the shirt, shaking him. "Where is Arturo camped?"

"Frio—" Then he fainted or died.

"Where's that—Frio?" he asked Rosa.

"There is a dry river called that. Maybe a day's ride north of here."

Slocum straightened and rose to his feet. Grasping the man's arm, he dragged him unceremoniously out of the doorway and left him in the dirt. Then he went out back and hauled the second corpse the same way through the jacal, to leave him beside his stiffening compadre.

They had horses somewhere nearby. From the doorway, he looked back at the three grieving women on their knees beside their dead friend.

"You must have heard them coming," Grandmother said, looking up at him.

"Yes. Too late to save her, but maybe the rest of you were saved."

"We were. You did the best you could. I know now that Camila was the woman I saw dead."

He stepped over, hugged her frail form. "I'm so sorry."

"No. We want to thank you so much."

"I would not be alive today were it not for you and them."

Grandmother excused herself to get ready for the funeral.

He and Rosa went in search of the horses. They found them hitched in a dry wash. At once, he let out the stirrups on the toughest-looking of the two mustangs and they rode them back to camp. The rig he chose was a big wooden-horned saddle, but the girth was near new and the leather looked all right.

He spent the day into afternoon digging the graves. A deep one was readied for Camila, and the other one was deep enough that the dogs wouldn't dig the the dead men's bodies up. The women took turns spelling him at the job until they reached the proper depth.

All the bodies were lowered into place, and Grand-mother said some final words and Hail Marys for Camila's ascension into heaven. Then, in the last light of the bloody sundown, worn out and exhausted, they staggered back to the jacal and ate reheated frijoles. Sometimes, people like Grandmother and the "lost" women around her suffered at the hands of such men as had ridden in looking for him, but mostly, he figured they all had peaceful days in which no one preyed on or abused them.

The next morning, he worked over the kac to be sure it was sound, and checked the horses' hooves. Without blacksmith tools, he couldn't shoe them, but he did cut their hooves down, and used a rasp Rosa had to smooth them so the horses would walk more up on their toes than their heels. They probably had not ever been shod. Many horses in Mexico never wore a steel plate. In the desert, they didn't particularly need them, but in the sharp gravel in the Madres, being shod or not could be a life-or-death situation for the rider.

"How are your eyes?" Rosa asked, gathering her skirts up in a wad and squatting beside him as he bent over rasping on a hoof in his lap.

"I'm seeing good."

"You have your strength back, too." She motioned to his work.

"Most of it."

"Can I go with you?"

"I don't think that would be a good idea. I may not survive this meeting. What would you do then?"

"You will survive. I know that. I could help you. I want those bastards. That bitch Francisca ran and told them you were here. I hope they paid her well. I catch her, I may stick a post up her ass."

"I can't say what might happen up there." Satisfied with his job on the hoof, he dropped the hoof and straightened his stiff back. Bent half backward, he began to swing his arms to try and loosen the tight muscles. "It's too dangerous."

"But I can show you the way,"

He chewed on his lower lip and studied the purple

mountains. "All right, but no trying to be brave. One dead woman is enough for this week."

"*Gracias.* When will we leave?"

"I'd leave here now if you know that area."

"We can go now," she said. "I am sure they are camped at the Vasquez ranch. The ranch owners are in Mexico City. The Apaches scared them away."

"They weren't the only ones." He hobbled the horse and followed her to the jacal.

"You are leaving?" Grandmother asked when he returned.

"Yes, soon."

"Be careful. These men are all bad killers."

"I know. They almost killed me."

"How are your eyes?"

"Good."

"May God ride with you, my son."

"I'll need him, I am certain." He hugged her and she blushed.

"Once, such a powerful man hugging me would have sent lightning to my brain. Now, all I get are concerns you might not return someday to see me again."

He looked around the yard. She had so little and was so rich in things that counted—making a home for the abused, bringing tranquillity to their lives in the midst of the turmoil that swirled around everyday life in Mexico.

He gave her some money for the bad days. Bought two blankets. One for Rosa and one for himself. The women cried some, hugging each other. Rosa soon broke away, carrying a small rug bag that she hung on the saddle horn as she mounted up. With a wave of good-bye, they rode north.

Day fell into twilight, then night. Stars came out, and the half-moon's appearance accompanied the night insects' sounds and the cooing of some birds in the chaparral, the soft clop of their unshod horses in the loose dust of the road underfoot, and an occasional snort of their animals. He listened keenly for any out-of-place noise.

In the predawn, they reined up on a rise and studied the darkranchero buildings. He wondered if he had time to scout the place and not get discovered before he had control of Arturo. It was a chance he had to take. He dismounted and gave Rosa the reins.

"Stay here. I don't come back, ride like hell out of here."

"I'll go with you. I can use a gun."

"No, see about the horses and if I can get her out, fine—otherwise, you ride the hell out of here."

She surrendered and agreed to his terms. He left her standing, and took off in a low run and reached the buildings. In the shadows, he controlled his breathing to regain his breath. Where was Meia?

Someone was stirring up the ashes. Was it Meia? On quiet soles, he rounded the building and caught the heavy smell of wood ashes being aroused. She was bent over, and he recognized her slender form and crossed to her with a hiss.

"Oh! You're alive—"

He pressed his hand to her mouth. "Be quiet and come with me."

With a quick check around, he pointed to the south, where he'd come from. "Go."

Hand on his gun butt, he whirled around looking for any opposition, then followed on her heels. Every step they took sounded loud as two elephants, but in seconds they were beyond the buildings and in the thin mesquite brush.

"How did you survive?" she whispered.

"Good care by Rosa here and her friends."

"Hello," she said to Rosa. "I knew he was dead."

"So did we when we first found him."

"Get on the horse with her and let's clear out. I don't have the manpower to fight them here," he said.

In seconds, they were headed south in a long trot. Once out of the outlaws' hearing, he asked Meia, "How many men does he have?"

"Five or six."

He nodded in the starlight. "We did the right thing then."

"Yes, but he will be mad."

"I don't give a damn."

Meia issued a nervous laugh riding behind Rosa on the horse. "I never figured that you did."

"Where will we go now?" Rosa asked.

"I need to learn all I can about an Apache. He has a white woman I am supposed to try and get out of his camp. Maybe you two should stay at Grandmother's."

"Arturo could find her there." Rosa shook her head in disapproval.

"Does he believe in your mine?" Slocum asked.

Meia nodded. "But he thinks, like the others, that it caved in and it would take lots of timbers and digging to even get inside, if that wasn't collapsed, too."

"So how shall we handle it?"

"I don't know. The mine is there. I swear there is gold in the mine. But I can trust so few. If I hired them to protect me, they'd soon rob me and perhaps even murder me."

"For now, we need to ride a ways and then make camp. We will need to take turns at guard because as you say, he'll come after you." What Slocum needed was a defensible place, and then he could get some rest and maybe some ideas about how to avoid Arturo. "Are we going toward the mine now?"

"We must turn east soon." Meia acted uncertain as she looked at the silhouettes of the mountain peaks around them.

"How far away is it?"

"Maybe fifteen miles."

"You can show us the way, take the lead."

"Isn't that dangerous, going there?"

"I'll figure that out. Right now, we have one pistol and enough ammo to hold them off for a little while. Are there any explosives at the mine?"

"Yes, why?"

"'Cause we can use them to hold off Arturo and his

men. By the way, did they have some enriched ore on those mules?"

"Yes, they stole it, too," Meia said.

"Figures why he wants to get into your mine. He wants more to take out. So when he rides out, he won't need to come back. Folks up here figure out that he's a thief, they won't ever trust him again to haul anything for them."

Both women agreed.

Slocum found a place he liked with only one narrow way up to it. On top, he and the two women dismounted and hobbled the horses, leaving them saddled in case—then he made the women go to sleep. He promised to wake them for the next shift. They must have been tired, for they obeyed him.

He sat on the ground, back to a ponderosa trunk, and looked over the starlit approach. From his vantage point, he could see anything that moved across the open country below. Maybe, maybe Arturo would only send a couple of men. Slocum's chances were better against two than four or all six men and their boss. *Divide and conquer them.*

The night crickets chirped and an owl called to its mate. The cool night air set in and he wished for a blanket, but the girls had them and needed them. He rubbed his shirt-sleeves and decided the coolness would keep him awake. A soft night wind swept through the boughs overhead and they made their own music.

How was Mrs. Ramsey?

12

Mrs. Ramsey hated being alone by herself in the night. The vastness of the mountains made her yearn to be back in her frame house. Every red wolf that howled on some ridge above her made cold chills run up her spine. Her knees drawn up to her chin and under the Navajo blanket to preserve her warmth, she waited and listened for the sound of either riders coming on her back trail or Ojo.

Times like this, she regretted her own foolishness and haste when she took to run off with Ojo. Only a crazy woman possessed with having real sex with an animal-like stallion would have done such a dumb thing. Maybe she'd had too long a time to think about it, with Onswell coming once every few months and having one night of grunt-and-pump sex with her.

Each time, when he was visiting her and they went to bed, he would push up her nightgown, then spread her legs apart. Being certain the sheet would cover them from anyone seeing their activities, he would begin taking his pleasure. Even that had become halfhearted for him since she'd never carried a child over three months. A barren woman was perhaps not worth his efforts anymore. She knew each time he came, he grew more and more anxious to get back to the fertile ones. A man with thirty-some living offspring could hardly waste his seed on a childless partner. He'd even threatened to give her place to Alma, his second wife, and move her back to St. David.

There, she'd never get him in her bed. His two new teenage wives would hoard his company, both big-bellied with their first to be born. Cousins that he claimed would marry him only if he took both of them. *The liar*.

No way she'd ever regret leaving Onswell—but if Ojo was dead, what could she do? There went that damn wolf again.

Did he know she was alone and defenseless? She shuddered and tried to rub the goose bumps off the back of her arms. Her twat had begun itch, too. She squirmed and crossed her legs. That was the cause of most of her problems. Hers was not an ordinary one; she had a definite need for it more often than most women.

At St. David, a few years earlier, she tried talk to Joanie, Ramsey's first wife, about *her condition* and fiery needs. The woman was so shocked that she told her she must pray harder for relief from it. That the devil had hold of her private spot like he had hold of others' hearts, and that she should ask the Lord for deliverance every hour until it ceased.

That never worked. No need to talk to the rest of those stiff sisters—they obviously had no problems like hers, and considered sex with their husbands merely an inconvenience imposed on them as Eve's descendants. Sometimes, her finger's action could do the trick. She untied the skirt at the waist and opened the front so that her flat hand could enter, slide over her lower belly, then feel the stiff pubic-hair-covered mound and crease. If only her efforts this time eased the itch for a little while—

No one came after them in the night. After taking their turn on guard, the two women woke Slocum in the predawn.

They ate some jerky and rode on. Food would soon be a problem. He had few supplies save the few things that Rosa had brought along.

Late evening, they watered at a large spring. The horses grazed and the three riders walked around to walk out the stiffness. Slocum went back and studied their back trail for any signs of pursuit or dust rising up. Nothing.

"Did he give up?" Meia asked upon his return.

"Arturo has a plan, you can count on that. Don't count him out."

They mounted up and rode into the valley that she said held her mine. It was a vast land of pine forest and open meadows. Every time they'd stirred up a mule deer or two, he hadn't been able to shoot, not wanting to alert their enemy where they might be at. It was now time to find a deer to eat.

One shot was all he dared use. No one could tell the direction of a single shot if he wasn't prepared for it. Two, and they could place his location. Suddenly, a yearling popped up from behind a large fallen log. The deer's mistake was he took time to arch his back and stretch before considering the intruders. The bullet dropped him.

For a long while, Slocum sat his horse and listened. Only the calling of some ravens could be heard on the afternoon wind. Rosa took his knife and used it to cut the deer's throat; then the two women dragged the carcass out by the hind legs.

"Kill a deer and there isn't a single tree around to hang him from," Meia said, and laughed.

Amused at her words, he twisted in the saddle, searching for a suitable tree. Then he swung down to the ground. "I'll load him and we'll ride over to the edge and find us a tree limb to hang him up on."

Both women helped him put the deer's carcass across the saddle. Good enough, but he still felt concerned about the shot attracting someone. It was down to shoot it or starve, and he felt the risk worth taking. At the edge of the wide meadow, he found a low enough branch to swing the carcass on, and the women went to skinning it out.

"I'm going to scout around. Keep your eyes out for any sign of Arturo."

They agreed, though they were busy talking, and he wondered how good they'd look out. Back in the saddle, he trotted the horse up to the north end of the clearing. No tracks, no signs. Good, but they were getting close to her mine. This big open spot had plenty of grass for their ponies, but they could be seen grazing a mile away.

He'd forgotten to ask Meia about the water situation at the mine. There was a small sluggish stream that meandered across the basin, leaving tules and marshy spots, but it wasan't an ideal water source for humans. He turned the horse around and headed back. Maybe Meia knew of a better one.

A small fire cooked the liver and kidneys on a spit. Both women were bloody to the elbows when they grinned at his return.

"Is there a place for you two to wash up and we can cool out that carcass?"

"See that side canyon?" Meia pointed to the rock cliffs that came in from the east. "There's plenty of water over there."

"I'll load that deer over a horse," he said. "You two can wash it out and cool it down over there. I'll look after the food cooking. Tie it high in a tree so no varmint can get it, and after supper tonight we'll move over there."

"Don't burn our supper." Rosa swung on his arm, and then laughed with Meia about the notion.

The deer was slung across the horse and the two women soon headed for the water source. His own pony was busy snatching bunchgrass by the mouthful. Good, he'd get his bellyful. Sunk on his haunches, Slocum reloaded the .44's cylinder. Be nice to have had the time and tools to clean it, but that would have to wait. Where was Arturo at?

He might be up at Meia's mine waiting for them. Slocum hadn't thought about it, but if that outlaw knew about the cave-in, more than likely he knew right where the mine was located. Where else would he wait but at the front door? They'd need to approach it more carefully than Slocum had imagined earlier. As he turned the meat on the spit, he wondered how long the women would be gone.

Everything took time, especially trail-dirty women with water to bathe in. Past sundown, he heard them coming back. The meat was cooked, and he'd considered taking one of the kidneys off and hiding the rest.

"Well, what's it taste like?" Rosa asked.

"I've been waiting for you two."

"Good," Meia said. "We thought you might have eaten it all."

"Not me."

"Good, then we have a reward for you."

"What's that?"

"One of us is going to sleep with you tonight."

"Sounds generous enough. Let's eat."

"Yes, you may need your strength." Meia shared some laughter with her companion.

They were already dividing him up. Rosa served him one of the kidneys on a bark dish, and they shared the other one, all three seated cross-legged in the twilight. The women both looked refreshed in the fire's light from their bath.

"I wondered, could Arturo be at the mine already?" he asked Meia.

"Oh, you think he went there?"

"I'm suspicious that he might have known that it would be our business to go there after rescuing you."

She paused in her eating and ran the back of her hand over her mouth. "We can go in the back way."

"We'll do that. How far is it from here?"

"Not over two hours."

"Just right."

"We'll go there next?" she asked.

Slocum agreed.

The moon was rising when he finished hobbling the horses at their new camp. He returned, stood over them, and unstrapped his gun belt. He wrapped it up and offered it to them. "Who's first guard?"

"Rosa," Meia said, and scrambled to her feet. "You ready now?"

"I want a bath, too," he said.

"Good. I hate dirty old men." They laughed aloud.

With her on his arm and the one towel in the outfit, he headed for the gurgling creek. She pointed out a pool that shone in the moonlight filtering through the pines on the slope. "That's waist deep," she said. "But it's real cold."

"I won't stay in long then," he said, toeing off his boots.

"I wasn't afraid it would shrink you, but then it might." She gave him a playful shove. "And since I won you for tonight, it might be my loss."

Stripped down, he reached over and cupped her chin to give her a quick kiss. He drew a big smile of approval from her. He felt her hand run down his bare side, and then he left, hobbling over the rocks for the creek.

The water proved breathtakingly cold. But he rubbed handfuls of sand on his skin until he felt clean all over, and then came sloshing out. She began to dry his back, and then he bent over for her to work on his hair. Soon, he straightened and she worked down.

"I forgot the blanket," she said in disgust on her knees, carefully drying his scrotum and half an erection, as if examining it. Then she took his dick in her mouth and used her tongue on the ring under the head. Jacking it slowly, she giggled. "I can bend over for you if that's all right?"

He caught her face in his hands, and the still-damp thick ringlets curled around his fingers. "Horny as I am right now, we can do it any way."

"Good. I'll remember next time." She bent over, exposing her slender butt toward him.

His hands on her narrow hips to steady her, he moved

tight against her, and she reached under and inserted his erection in her gates, moving against him for more of it. Damn—she felt good he was inside her. He hunched himself deeper.

Before the cool daybreak, they ate the leftover liver and heart and they took the deer carcass with them. Meia promised to lead them in the back way, and he planned to hide their horses way short of the mine. A horse could be noisy coming off a rocky mountain, and they needed the element of surprise on their side. The way was straight up and probably only used by mountain sheep. Halfway there, they rested their backs against tree trunks and caught their short wind in the high elevation.

"Almost there," Meia promised.

He accepted her words with a nod and they went on again. The crest was still high above them in the thick timber. His lungs ached, his temples pounded, and the women were out of breath as well, but they strove on.

At last, she signaled the mine was over this last mountain. He swung the deer up in a tree, and the women hobbled their mounts. Meia led the way up the steep game trail. The gravel crunched under their feet. He kept an eye out for any sign, and they soon dropped down on their bellies, muffling any coughing.

There, in the meadow far below, were several of Arturo's mules grazing and honking at one another.

"You guessed it," Meia said in a half whisper. "They're at the caved-in entrance."

"What now?" Rosa asked.

"Can we get to the explosives from here?" Slocum asked.

Meia nodded. "They are in the other mine entrance. I think we can find them."

"Where's that?"

"More left of here and if we keep low, they won't see us."

"Good. Lead the way."

They stayed bent over, moving across the ridge and listening to the men cussing beneath them. Their voices carried in the deep canyon more than they could ever imagine. Slocum frowned at the sight of an outhouse sitting by itself so high up above the timber and such a climb up from the mine.

"What's this?" Rosa asked.

"The doorway to the mine," said Meia

"How does that work?" Rosa scowled at Slocum.

He turned up his palms at her.

"Listen to me," Meia said. "The ladder going down is a long one. Be careful. The fall would kill you."

"Who uses this outhouse?" Rosa asked.

"No one, but it makes a perfect cover." Meia opened the door and motioned for him to come forward. "The floor lifts up here."

He nodded and found the edge. Sure enough, a trapdoor lifted up short of the box that one sat on.

"I'm not certain—" Rosa said.

"I have no light up here," Meia warned her. "There's lamps down there, but it's a long ways down there."

"You want to stay up here?" Slocum asked Rosa.

"No. But I hate mines and dark places."

"You decide," he said.

"Shit," Rosa swore. "I wish I'd had you last night instead of her having you. I'm sitting on the edge anyway." Her shoulders gave a shudder and she hugged him out of impulse.

He patted her back and nodded. "Don't think about it."

"Don't think about what? The craving that's got me in a fever, or falling to my death in her shithouse?"

"I'm sorry, Rosa," Meia said. "Think about how rich we'll be when this is over."

"Oh, I'd pay a fancy price for it right here and now." She peeked over in the dark shaft and drew back.

"Time to decide," Slocum said, holding the lid open.

Chewing on her lip, she drew a deep breath and then crossed herself. "Mother of God help me."

Meia went first and he pulled the outside door of the outhouse shut when Rosa scrambled inside and started down. Astraddle the hole, he let them get down a ways, knowing he was going to shut most of the light off; then he began his descent and closed the lid down on top of his head.

"Oh—" Rosa gave a cry. "There better be millions in gold down here. I mean millions—"

The ladder was well made, but it groaned in places and creaked threateningly in other places. Engulfed by complete darkness, he could not see anything and had no idea how far the wall was behind him. Step by step, being careful not to step on Rosa's hands, he let himself down. Stopped for a second, he felt the updraft coming from below. Good, the mine must breathe. That knowledge made him feel easier. Many mines became death traps of bad air, especially when the entrance was closed.

"Rosa, there is a platform we can stop and stand on halfway down," Meia said in a soft voice.

"I may pee on you—damn, I knew this would be bad—"

"Take your time," he cautioned. "We'll be fine."

"You and her maybe. I'll probably die down here."

"No one's dying but those damn bandits," he said, sharper than he intended. This business was getting to him, too.

"I'm sorry—"

"I know. Think positive."

"I will. I will, I promise."

That settled, he went down some more and stopped, realizing his feet were down to her hands.

"It's the platform," she said.

"Fine," he said, and moved down beside her. When his boots were at last on the firm platform and his arms were hugging both of them, he felt their body tremors under his palms.

They were halfway.

13

Deep into her own pleasure, Mrs. Ramsey raised her butt off the rocks under her toward her persistent finger, which was busy teasing her stiff erection and then plunging in the aching void. This wasn't her first time to arouse herself, but it proved to be a better one than most. Her breathing grew deeper and her hand movements faster, until at last the tight string broke and a flush of fluids rushed into her hand. Depleted, she collapsed in a semi-faint.

Shielding her face with her straw hat from the too bright sun, she worked to close her skirt and cover up her exposed parts while lying on the hillside. Had her man lived through the surprise attack? Only time would tell.

On her feet, she staggered to the horse. Belly down, she squirmed to get on him again. The gooey wetness in her crotch was not that uncomfortable considering the ease she felt after doing it.

How far must she go to find someone or have them find her? There were other Apache bands in the Madres. They might take her in if she stumbled across them. But that was not something to think about. Most Apache would consider raping her as a way to get even with her people for what the soldiers did to their women. Women were merely sticklike figures to most men. The soldiers raped the Apache women, the Apache men raped back. It was a never-ending source of trouble in this land.

She nudged the horse downhill into the valley. May be water there, and she could use some—even more than food. Though her empty stomach growled in protest to the horse shifting her around on his back, she headed off the mountain.

Where was Ojo, if he was even alive?

Standing flat-footed on the mine's floor at last, Slocum struck the first gopher match, and the light illuminated the piles of supplies and kegs of blasting powder. Meia had brought a candle lamp, and they soon had light in the low-roofed shaft.

"See this?" she said, holding up a rusty helmet from a conquistador. "My husband always thought it was an old Spanish mine."

"May have been. How long is the mine?" he asked, holding the lamp up to see as much as he could.

"Follow me," Meia said to him.

"Don't leave me," Rosa said, struggling back to her feet. Looking all around, she hugged herself as if cold, though the mine felt comfortable to him.

They went less than thirty feet, and Meia pointed to the vein of gold in the wall. Over four inches thick, the yellow precious metal glowed in the lamplight.

"See, I told you I had gold."

He whistled at the size of the vein and then shook his head. "How thick is the collapsed part?"

"He estimated ten feet. He had the money on him to hire the help. There were supposed to be six men coming with him as guards, but I think they were the ones robbed and killed him for the money he had on him."

Rosa shook her head. "You can't trust anyone."

"Somewhere, there are men true to their word that would

be loyal," said Slocum. "Trouble is, there are bastards out looking for deals like this to take the gold and run."

"Find me those men true to their word," Meia challenged him.

"We can take enough high-grade ore out to hire them," Slocum said.

"Where will you go to find them?"

"Dolgres. There is a man by the name of McNeal there. He can hire you honest men that would fight for you and your mine. This trip, we can get enough gold out of here to do that and buy the supplies you will need."

"Dolgres is a long ways from here," Rosa said.

He hugged her shoulder. "Nothing is handy."

"That is so. What do we do now?"

"Load some sticks of blasting powder. We are going to have Fourth of July with Arturo."

"Let's get it done—rich or poor, I hate this tunnel." Rosa shook her head in disbelief.

"You are rich," Meia said. "I promised you a third and him a third."

"Wish I could stay, but I can't," he said. "So you girls share the mine fifty-fifty."

"You mean you'd turn your back on this fortune?" Meia blinked in disbelief at him.

"Darling, I love both of you, but I gave my word to a man called Crook that I'd try to find a white woman held hostage by an Apache. Cost me one good Apache scout so far. I'm still going to do that."

"But we need you."

"We're going to get the gold out that you two need. I'm going to get rid of Arturo shortly, and then I'm going to swing up on the Blanco and look for that woman. I have to give it my all—I promised a man I'd do that much."

"Where will we be while you are gone?" Rosa asked.

"Hiding out at Grandmother's. No one will know you have gold on you. Just another trip in here to look for it is all you say. I'll finish the white hostage job and I'll join you."

"Who is she?" Meia asked. "This grandmother?"

"The one I told you about," Rosa reminded her.

"What if you can't find her—this hostage?" Meia asked him.

"I'll give up and come get you girls."

Rosa giggled. "Don't be gone too long, we both like you."

Meia agreed.

"Good. Now, blasting sticks. Get some out of those unbroken cases. I'm taking Arturo out with them. But first we must load them—carefully. I'll show you how."

Seated on the ground, they began arming the sticks. The women made him a backpack to carry them up the ladder, and when all was done, they began the ascent.

"Now, I want one of you to get close to his mules and let a stick off near them. The other one goes to the opposite side of camp and tosses in a few for good luck. Keep them off guard and dancing. It will be over quickly."

"You sound so sure this will work," Rosa said from behind him.

"It has every other time I used it. Why not this time?"

"You probably had hard-core men helping you, not two rich *putas.*" Rosa sounded uncertain.

"We can be rich now, can't we?" Meia said. "Rich enough to do what we want."

"And screw who we want as well." Rosa laughed.

"To the gold!"

"Hush," he said to them. "This ain't over—yet."

When the women fell silent, he went hand over hand up the wooden rungs. Soon, he paused below the lip and listened. No sound. He used his shoulder to lift the floor, and in a few seconds had it up and open.

"Stay there," he said, and peeked out the front door through the cracks. Nothing was in sight. He swung it open and, satisfied, reached down to pull Rosa out by the wrist. She gasped in relief, going out the open door on her hands and knees. Meia came right after her.

"You all right?" Meia asked, putting her hand on the upset girl's shoulder.

"I-I think so."

"What do we do now?" Meia asked Slocum.

"Wait till dark, then sneak down there and have a party with Arturo."

"We better not cook anything, right?"

"Don't want him to know a thing about what's coming." He swung the backpack down on the ground.

Rosa was sitting up on her butt cross-legged, and combed her hair back with her fingers. "I hope even if we are rich, I don't have to make many more of those trips."

"When we get Arturo taken care of, we will have to haul up some gold. I figure it will take us a few days to pick it out and then haul it up here."

"I'll be glad to see him gone for what he's done to Meia and others," Rosa said, bobbing her head and struggling to get up. "I hope those no-accounts down there have supper waiting for us when we get through with them."

"Wouldn't be a bad idea." He put the outhouse floor back in place and closed the front door, and then he used some dry brush to wipe out any of their tracks.

"I never thought of that," Meia said, hands on her hips, looking impressed. "I need to remember that."

He smiled at her. "You won't fool an Apache, but you might a Mexican or a gringo."

Twilight set in, and they crept up on Arturo's camp. Each woman had gopher matches and carried five explosives that were tied on sticks so they could throw them farther. He warned them that some might fizzle out, and to be ready to throw another one hard at the camp and then duck the percussion. Rosa was set to spook the mules with hers. Meia was to toss at least one explosive in the campfire. Besides his own, he had his six-gun, and he told the women that they needed the outlaws' guns as bad as anything.

His greatest hope was that the blasting attack would make the outlaws give up. It had worked before. Maybe this time. Depended how hardened they were. Meia had never said much about her time in their camp, except earlier she'd said that Arturo had raped her. But from what little he'd heard from Rosa, Meia's second time as his victim hadn't been good at all.

When Slocum was in place, he hooted like a owl. In forty seconds, the blast went off and stampeded the mules right through camp. When Meia's stick hit their campfire, as the mules were leaping over and tromping on several howling men in their frantic effort to escape, the fire and ashes shot high in the air.

"Mother of God!" the men shouted. "We give up, hombres!"

"Fight, you sonsabitches! Fight!" Arturo shouted from among his men.

Slocum lit another explosive and tossed it in the man's direction. The blast went off and more screams followed. Armed with rifles they'd secured from the outlaws, the two women advanced on the camp. Some of the men tried to crawl away. Others, scooting on their butts, tried to move back.

"Where is Arturo?" Meia demanded, looking over the broken outlaws with their hands held high. Most were seated on their butts, looking wide-eyed in the starlight at the victors.

"They are only fucking *putas*," one said in disgust.

"Where is he? Where is Arturo?" Slocum shouted.

No answer. He became more frantic. Even if they had all the rest, how had the leader escaped? Slocum had to have him. It was like a wounded rattler you shared a cave with—even wounded, he could bite you.

He saw that Meia had one outlaw on his hands and knees. She demanded he pull down his pants, and when at first he did not move, she gouged him hard in the side with her rifle.

"You remember shoving the barrel of your pistol in my ass?" she demanded.

"No. No. It wasn't me."

"Get those pants down. Now!"

He reached back, and soon bared his ass to her.

"Bend over."

"Oh, please—"

"Now tell me how this feels, huh?"

"It hurts bad—"

"I told you so, didn't I?"

"*Sí,* but—" His hysterical screams cut the night when she drove the rifle barrel in his butt. "Take it! Take it out! Mother of God you are killing me."

"You want some more like this?"

"Oh, no. No."

"You asked me that, didn't you?"

"*Sí, sí.* Oh, please, oh, please, take it out."

"When I pull the trigger?"

"No. No."

Rosa had the others corralled in a bunch. Each acted afraid that he might be the next one tortured. Slocum took off to find Arturo. He looked under the low boughs of the junipers, and could see nothing in the last light of twilight. Then he heard some gravel churning on the mountain from someone or something scrambling to get away. Arturo—no doubt.

He charged up the trail, looking around and wishing for more light. Then, out of nowhere, a fecal-breathed madman reared up, screaming and jumping at him—a knife blade shone in his hand. The blade cut Slocum's shirtsleeve at his shoulder. Then the attacker lost his balance and went rolling downhill.

Slocum took up pursuit, going stiff-legged down the slope, and found Arturo downhill with his own knife stuck in his chest and gasping for air. "You bastard. You bastard . . . you and those dumb women beat me . . ."

"You're the stupid one . . ."

14

Mrs. Ramsey found a camp of miners. Five small, filthy men who huddled around a twig fire waiting for their frijoles to cook. Not one even raised an eye when she rode in and dropped from her horse.

"My name is Señora Ramsey. My husband will pay a large sum of money for my safe return to the border."

No one moved. All of them looked so dirt-crusted, they resembled statues more than living men. Even their eye movements were slow, as if their minds were dull.

"Anyone talk English?" she asked.

No answer.

"Español?"

No answer.

Finally, one man rubbed his hand over his mouth and nodded. "We are Yacquis, not Messikins."

"Good. I need to get to the border. It is very important."

"We are not going to the border today," he said.

"Not even for a lot of money?"

He shook his head. "Not today or tomorrow. But you are welcome to eat with us."

If the cook was as dirty as the others looked, she wondered if the food would be safe. But her belly button was scraping her spine. Better to eat than die of hunger.

"Thank you."

"Come and sit in a place of honor. We seldom have guests up here."

She agreed, wondering how many would attend such a meal with such solemn, filthy people. Where was Ojo?

When the dust settled, Slocum figured out only three of Arturo's bunch had survived, including the one Meia had poked in the ass with the gun barrel. Slocum made them dig graves while the women guarded them with rifles. Under the starlight, he rounded up the mules that had not run far from camp, and soon found the bell mare.

When he returned, he only tied the mare up. The mules wouldn't leave her anyway.

"The dead ones are planted," Meia said, coming to meet him.

He dismounted heavily. "You look in the panniers yet?"

She shook her head.

"We better have a look-see." He noticed that Rosa had the three prisoners seated on the ground.

"We'll be back," he told her, and they went over to the packs. As he suspected, the first one they opened under the light of his match was rich in raw silver and gold ore. He began to dig aside the loose high-grade material, and his fingers soon closed on an ingot. He never drew it out. No one's business. There was no tax at the U.S. border on ore that needed to be smelted, but there was a tariff on the refined stuff. Clapping his hands over the open pannier to put any gold dust on his hands back in, he nodded in approval.

"The owners of this treasure no doubt are dead. There's plenty enough gold here to open and operate your mine."

"Good. Rosa will be glad. She won't have to go down there again."

Slocum chuckled.

Back by the campfire, Rosa sidled over to him and in a half whisper asked, "What did you find?"

"Enough."

She frowned at him with impatience. "Enough what?"

"Enough gold and silver to open your mine."

"Good."

"What will we do with them?" Meia asked with a head toss at the prisoners.

"Should have shot them, I guess. Taking prisoners always makes it hard. There is no law up here. Besides, if you turned them in to some officials, they'd want the treasure for themselves." He shook his head wearily "We'll load up tomorrow and abandon them somewhere. They'll make it out fine. They don't, they shouldn't have joined his gang."

"Good enough. We better tie them up for tonight, huh?" Meia asked.

"I'll do that," he said, and went to find some rope.

She located a lamp and carried it as a light for him as he bound up the grumbling outlaws. Slocum had no time for their bitching, and shoved them facedown and tied them. When he finished, Slocum and the women sat cross-legged on the ground and ate some jerky washed down with coffee that Rosa had made.

"My turn to pull guard first," Meia said.

"My turn to share you." Rosa grinned big at him.

"Oh, yes. It is your turn," Meia said. They both laughed.

"You can mend his torn shirt, too, while you guard them," Rosa said, pointing out the slash Arturo had made in the sleeve.

Slocum glanced down at his sleeve. Lucky that Arturo had missed him.

"Take it off," Meia said with a tone of disgust. "I can fix it."

He did, and then left with Rosa. She acted anxious to get him away from there. But she was always anxious, especially when it involved sex.

Minutes later with him on top of her poking it to her, she

looked up in the starlight at him. "I wish you'd stay with us forever. I could share you with five women. Oh, Mother of God, you feel so damn good."

He took the second guard shift, and sat out with the hoot owls. The prisoners snored and so did the mules. He felt grateful, too, when the Big Dipper told him it was time for him to wake Rosa.

In the predawn, he had to use a twitch on each mule to make them hold still. It was a loop of chain on a stick that wrapped up on a mule's upper lip to force him to stand to be packed. Rosa did the twisting while he put on the pack-saddle and then loaded the heavy panniers. He could have used one of the prisoners, but he didn't trust them.

Soon, the mules were loaded and Meia had food for the three of them and some corn mush made for the prisoners. Slocum untied them and told them to eat fast. Meanwhile, he tied a reata around each of their necks so they would be in a chain and could be led.

"One wrong move and we'll drag you to your death. Savvy?" he asked when he finished.

They grunted and dug into their porridge.

"You going to tie their hands in back?" Meia asked when he came over to their side of the fire.

He shook his head. "They know if I tie them up, they will die with that reata around their necks if they fall. They won't try anything."

"How far is Dolgres and this man McNeal?" Meia asked.

"Four hard days' ride."

"What about that woman you came after?"

"She will have to wait. She's waited this long."

"You know we love you and appreciate all you do for us. Why you can't stay with us is beyond me. We're—" She lowered her voice. "Rich."

"I know and it pains me. But once you two are in safe hands, I must try to find the American woman."

"Is she pretty?"

"That's not it. I gave my word to a man I like and respect that I'd try to find her."

She nuzzled her face in his shirt and hugged him. "I'd make you my prisoner."

"Let's ride. The days will be long."

"My night tonight," she reminded him.

He nodded in agreement. She might be too tired by then to want to do a damn thing but sleep. They had lots of ground to cover, and the way out was no soft dream either.

"How much money do we have?" she asked as he boosted her in the saddle.

"A king's ransom." He shook his head. More than he could count, that was for certain.

"Rosa, you lead the prisoners. Meia, you ride in back and shoot the first one that tries anything. I'll take the mules and the lead." He rode in close to Rosa and spoke softly. "Wrap that reata on your horn so if they fall off the cliff you can let them go."

In shock, she blinked her eyelashes at him, then swallowed hard. *"Sí."*

He dismounted and handed her the lead. "Here, drag them to their death."

At his words, the prisoners all pleaded aloud for her mercy.

Seated on his horse, he looked the three over. "Then you must keep up and not try anything."

He rode over, leaned forward, and jerked loose his tie on the bell mare's rope. "We're off."

When he put his heels to the horse, that meant they were headed out of the mother mountains so he could put the girls' gold in a safe place. A short while later, they reached a clearing in the forest and he looked up at the peaks. He hoped Mrs. Ramsey was still alive.

The trails off the mountain were tough, with wall-clinging narrow ledges. His left boot scuffed the sheer rock face, and the other stirrup hung out over open space for eagles.

"Don't look down," he said to the girls over his shoulder.

But telling them that was like telling a little kid not to put his tongue in the new space caused by losing a tooth. Over the clap of hooves on the trail, he heard one of them suck in her breath at what she saw. Probably Rosa. Meia was no doubt accustomed to these trails from going in and out with her husband to and from the mine.

This would be one of the fastest routes down, and he didn't mean going off the side either. An eerie sense set in his gut as the day wore on with little but a short stopover at some curve to break the journey. When they finally reached a mesa top, the girls dropped out of the saddle and about collapsed, then struggled up and ran, skirts in hand, for the security of some junipers to squat behind and empty their bladders.

The prisoners sunk on the ground, moaning. Slocum paid them little heed, and strode over to the next rim, thirty feet away, and scanned the trail going down ahead for any traffic. Nothing in sight. He stopped and pissed off the edge. By dark, they'd be in the foothills, and they could make some good time heading for Dolgres once they reached the desert.

The prisoners he'd turn loose somewhere soon. They were worthless riff-raff, but he didn't want them interfering with his delivery of the ore and ingots to a strong, secure bank. In the desert, he and the girls would still run the risk of meeting up with the bands of outlaws that roamed the land down there. But one thing at a time, he figured.

At the next stop, short of the foothills on a wide landing, he told the prisoners they were free to go.

"But what of these ropes we wear?" one asked.

"Maybe you will wear them out," he said.

"But we have no food or water, Señor."

"When you attacked me and left me for dead, did you worry about me?"

No one answered.

"You ever cross my path again, I'll kill you. Do you understand?"

"*Sí,*" they said in suppressed voices.

"Give each one a fistful of jerky," he said to Rosa, and turned to face the late afternoon sun. Better than they'd done for him. That completed, Slocum and the girls rode at a hard trot westward, the girls taking turns beating the mules on the butt to make them keep up. Their speed made the dust boil up, but he wanted miles between him and those men. By sundown, they reached a small stream, and the dust-floured women dropped heavily from their saddles and plunged in the knee-deep water. They plowed wakes with their skirts to get out in the stream, and finally fell to their knees in the deepest water. They used handfuls of water to wash their burning faces as Slocum watched them while watering the thirsty mules and horses.

The girls soon undressed and washed all their clothing in the stream. Then they came wading out, naked and stark brown, bronzed by the lowering sun, and hung their clothing on bushes. Naked as Eve, they both came to where he had started a fire.

"Feel better?" he asked, looking up from feeding the blaze into a larger one. They stood with their arms across their breasts, looking down at him. Their feet were in Mexican sandals braided out of some tough grass. He nodded in approval—one skinny woman with a small patch of black pubic hair, and one with a little more belly and fuller breasts than the other one. A man could do much worse for *campañeros*. One of them would want to share his blankets after the meal—how could he complain?

"We thought this might be the Garden of Eden," Meia said.

"It isn't, but I'll go wash, too, if you girls will cook us some supper."

"I'll do that. Rosa can wash your clothes while you bathe."

"Good. I'll do it just as soon as I unload the mules."

"Fine."

Rosa went with him. She helped undo the hitches and sweep off the canvas covers. He set the heavy panniers in a ring on the ground, and she stripped off the mules' saddles. The mules were tired enough that they had set aside their cranky ways of sunrise. With the bell mare hobbled and the animals turned out to graze, he was ready to bathe.

At the edge of the water, he undressed, and she took his clothing out in the stream to wash it. He used handfuls of silt from the bottom to scrub his body, and soon felt cleaner and a little fishy smelling. They walked back to camp together.

"How many more days is it to this place?" Rosa asked.

"Maybe two or three."

She nodded. "I can hardly wait."

"Same here," Meia said, bent over the food with her small butt stuck in the air.

"I may be wrong on the time, but it is a considerable distance to Dolgres."

"What is the most dangerous part?" Meia asked.

"Every mile between here and there."

They agreed with a solemn nod.

Later in the bedroll, with him on top of the skinny Meia, she pulled him down and whispered in his ear, "Teach us about guns tomorrow."

"Okay," he said, and then shoved his piston deeper in her. Damn, she was a tight piece of ass.

Somewhere, a red wolf howled, and she wrapped her legs around him. In a minute, Rosa came over, dragging her bedroll. "I'm sorry to bother you two, but that damn wolf howling gives me goose bumps."

"Get in here," Meia said, patting the blankets. "We're only using half of it."

They all three laughed.

15

Being among the almost silent Yacqui miners was different for her. They paid Mrs. Ramsey little attention and, even at meals, they treated her like she was a princess. They wouldn't even let her cook, and told her to stay under the grass-roofed ramada during the daytime. The older man called Guy, who did the cooking, braided her some sandals that fit her feet. Her rawhide knee boots were worn out, and she was grateful enough that she hugged him for the gift.

The third day, three men arrived with two mules loaded with rifles. These men were mustached Mexicans under large sombreros, and they stole hard looks at her. The kind of inspection that made the skin on the back of her neck crawl.

A trade was made for the rifles, and the gunrunners were paid in gold nuggets. She had no idea how much gold they received, but she felt the Mexicans were overpaid for the rifles and ammunition.

The leader of the miners, Two-gah, came over and squatted beside her. "These men will give us five rifles for you, but I don't think you want to leave with them. We can of course use the five new rifles in the fight for the return of our homeland, but we won't sell anyone into slavery. Too many of our people are dying in mines who were sold as slaves."

"I would like to remain here rather than go with them," she said softly. Her stomach cramped with sharp pains at the thought of what the gun traders would do to her.

"No," he said aloud to the Mexicans. "She wishes to stay here."

They looked angry at his answer, but all of the miners had loaded their new weapons, and so the Mexicans quickly smiled and tipped their sombreros at her. When they rode away, she knew they would not forget an American woman in a camp full of dusty *indios*.

"Could you write a letter for me?" the leader later asked her.

"My Spanish is poor. But I could write it in English."

"That would be a way to make it secret even if it fell in the wrong hands." He smiled at her. "Tomorrow we can write it. I must tell my chief about our new arms."

"Those men robbed you charging that much gold for those guns," she said, taking a chance on guessing the amount they were charged.

"I know, but the Americans won't let us bring guns into Mexico. We need these rifles."

"What will you do with them?"

"Long ago, we lived in a rich land on a strong river bearing our name and close to the west coast. Rich Mexican landowners now hold it. We want it back. Many of my people work in America to earn money for weapons."

"I see," she said.

"Tomorrow we write the letter. *Gracias, mi amiga.*" He started to leave.

"Two-gah, thanks for not selling me to those men. I didn't know I was worth so much money."

"*No problema, señora.*" He threw her a salute and went to talk to the men.

Good, maybe her man was still alive and had simply not found her yet. She would pray for his return some more.

The mules were loaded and on their way before daylight. Slocum's fresh-looking women made the mules trot hard by riding in and busting them with the tail ends of their reatas whenever they started to slack. This made for a fast-moving outfit, Slocum figured. He'd cut down two of the outlaws' holsters to fit the women's waists. Over breakfast, he'd explained how a six-gun worked. It had to be cocked to shoot. Hammer pulled back, and then trigger pulled.

They had the first-day-gun-wearing fidgets, moving the weapons around on their waists a lot to find comfortable places for them to ride. They also practiced drawing them. He wished he had some thirty-caliber guns for them to pack. The .44s were damn heavy, even in a man's hand, and kicked hard when fired. Later, he'd change them out for smaller-caliber revolvers.

The day grew more heated in the foothills they crossed over, but he kept them moving, expecting to make over forty or fifty miles a day with his caravan. They stopped twice to water themselves and their animals at the infrequent streams coming off the mother mountains, a luxury the desert ahead would not provide as easily.

The golden sunset shone on the bell tower of the church in San Paulo when they rode off the last rise. He slowed the train down to a stiff walk, and they entered the village gates. The unshod hooves clapped on the cobblestone paving. Yellow curs barked at them. Some goats bleated, and a jackass or two raised his raspy voice to join the mules in a chorus.

Slocum reined up at a cantina and slipped off his horse, handing his reins and lead to Meia. "I'll be right back. I know a man in this town who will lodge us."

She shared a nod with Rosa.

He pushed in the batwing doors and walked over to the

bar. The mustached bartender came down the polished bar to greet him.

"Doesn't a man named Porter live here?" Slocum said, and the man nodded.

"He lives on the hill in a big house."

"Gracias," Slocum said, and slapped two ten-centavo coins on the bar.

"You are passing through, Señor?"

"Sí," Slocum told him. Porter still lived there. It was none of that nosy hombre's business what Slocum was doing. Besides, the less said about this gringo, his two women, and a pack train, the better Slocum would like it. Outside, he mounted and he led the way up the crooked street. They cast long shadows over their shoulders.

He stopped at a tall gate, and then booted his horse up to use his revolver butt as a door knocker. Then, looking up through the red bougainvillea flowers and vines, he saw the familiar round red face of Homer Porter appear on a a balcony. He was dressed in a white bathrobe.

"Who's there?"

"An old amigo called Slocum."

"You are still alive?" he shouted.

"Open the gate and you can come down and take my pulse."

Porter shook his shiny face. "Juan. Juan, show our guests inside. I'll be right down."

The gate creaked open on heavy hinges, and the pleasant face of the yard keeper, Juan, smiled big as he admitted them with a bow. "Welcome. Welcome."

"I'll put the mules in the pen and unload them later," Slocum said to Juan.

"No, Señor. My boys and I can do that for you."

"Fine, but the panniers are very heavy to unload."

Juan shut the gate, saying, "We are strong, too."

"Hitch the horses, ladies. The man said he had help to put them up."

Meia smiled at Slocum as she dismounted. "Maybe we should kiss him for his efforts."

Slocum laughed. "All tips accepted."

Porter rushed out the front door and hugged him. "Why have you been away so long?"

"I want you to meet two business friends of mine."

"Ladies!" He bowed to them.

"I see why you have not been by to visit me. You are in the company of two lovely ladies. My dears, go right inside that door and Estela will show you to the baths and find you some robes to wear while your clothing is drying."

"Gracias," they said, and they joined the woman in the doorway.

"How long can you stay?" he asked Slocum in a whisper.

"One night."

"Why so short?"

"We need to meet a man in Dolgres. And I don't want to draw too much attention to us going through here."

Porter turned his head to the side as if suspicious of something. "Ah, you are in trouble again? Or they are?"

"We don't want to be looked at too hard, okay?"

"Fine. I'll point you in the direction of the baths, and then you and the girls join me for some good whiskey in the dining room. We have some delicious pork roast."

"Sounds wonderful."

He left Porter talking to his kitchen staff about supper, and walked down the hall. He knocked on the door, and the gray-headed Estela answered it. "They are both—"

"They've seen me. I've seen them. It'll be all right," he said.

"Of-of course, sir." She stepped back.

The two women were seated in copper tubs with bubbles up to their chins. They laughed. "He's okay."

"Good thing that Porter likes baths. There is still another tub not being used," Slocum said, and began undressing.

"Actually there are four tubs," Estela said with a wink. "And I have seen them all full."

"Porter is some kind of a bathhouse nut," Slocum said. "Got it from reading Roman history books. They must have taken lots of baths."

Estela brought over two pails of steaming water. She poured them in and he eased himself down in the hot water. It was hot enough to cook his gonads. But the muscle tightness began to leave his shoulders and back. Damn, this felt good. Maybe hot baths weren't such a bad idea after all. The girls were standing in their tubs and being rinsed off.

The two women left in their Turkish robes, chattering away. Estela came with a soap cup and razor. Without a word, she took a seat beside him and began to use the soapy bristle brush on his face. She was an expert with a straight razor, and he winked at her when she began slicing his whiskers away.

"You always were a stallion, but I bet those two can wear you out." She wiped the blade clean on a towel in her lap and continued shaving him. "If they don't have enough for you, then you know where my room is at."

"Gracias," he said when she finished.

She pinched his nose between her fingers playfully, then washed his face. "You are something else."

"Ike Clanton's man McCory. Is he in the area?"

"I have not heard of him lately."

"Good."

She paused, holding a pail in her hands, looking shocked at him. "You dodging McCory?"

He shook his head and stood up. Water rushed off him, and she went after a bucket of rinse water, stood on the chair, and dumped it on his head. "He better not get you. I'd miss you and your pet," she said.

"Next time I come through, I promise you," he said, taking a towel from her.

"No, you won't. Your buddy Porter will give you some young *puta* wilder than a deer and twice that good in bed."

They both laughed and then he reached out, took her by the arms, and kissed her hard on the mouth. When he was through, she pushed him away with both hands. "You'll be having me on my knees giving you a blow job next."

"Hmmm."

They both laughed.

"Oh, tell Juan that I want to be ready early in the morning, loaded and gone by sunrise."

She agreed, stood on her toes, and pecked his cheek.

Slocum found Porter and the two women on the second floor. Porter had the girls drinking strong liquor by the time he joined them in the spacious living room.

"He says we should stay here and rest a few days," Rosa said, waving her glass at the fine leather furniture and expensive art on the walls.

Slocum shook his head. "We can come back and do what the hell we want. The sooner this mission is over, the sooner the skin will quit crawling up the back of my neck. No, we leave here at sunrise."

Rosa wrinkled her nose at him and Meia laughed. "I told you what he'd say."

"What is your business to have acquired all this?" Rosa asked Porter before taking a deep draught from her glass.

"Diamonds. I am a dealer in diamonds."

"But you have no strong guard here. No one to protect them."

"Oh, I don't keep them here. They are all in the bank vault in town."

"When I am rich, will you make me a ring?"

"It will be my pleasure, madame."

"You look very nice," Meia said to Slocum, patting a place beside where she sat for him to sit.

"I feel clean anyway." He wore a white robe like the others. He took the place she suggested.

"Ah, whiskey for Slocum," Porter said, and delivered him a glass half full of the tea-colored liquor. "To better days in Mexico." He raised a toast.

They joined him.

Soon, a boy brought a guitar and sat down in the corner

on the floor. Softly, he began to play a ballad. Porter danced with Rosa, and his hand soon fell down on her butt and he pulled her to him. They swept around the tile floor with her body pressed against him. She carried her drink in her hand behind his back, and downed a sip every once in a while.

Meia laid her head on Slocum's shoulder. "You said early."

"Damn early."

"Those two can dance. Let us go to bed."

"Fine with me."

"You two leaving?" Porter asked over his shoulder while whirling Rosa across the tiles.

"Yeah, good night."

Out of Porter's hearing going down the hall, Meia chuckled. "He's a funny little man—Porter, I mean."

"I saved him once from a band of outlaws who were torturing him to find out where he kept his diamonds. He always has been grateful. I stay here when I come through."

"Why doesn't he have a mistress or wife?"

"It's a long story, but when those outlaws tortured him, they mutilated his manhood so badly that afterwards the doctor said he must lose what was left of it or die."

"Oh. Then he can't?"

"Not conventional-like."

"I'm sorry. He is so rich and yet—"

"He's alive. Him and Rosa will have fun. He can please a woman in his own ways."

"Whew. People are cruel to each other. I bet they were that cruel to my poor husband trying to get him to tell about the mine."

"Probably were."

"How many more days to Dolgres?"

"If we push hard—two."

"We must have come a long ways today."

"Yes, we pushed to get here."

She opened his robe, pressed her slender form to him, and hugged him. "I appreciate you."

He combed his fingers through her thick hair. "So far it's been a ball."

Shrugging off her robe, she let it drop and squeezed her body against his. "Let's get in bed. I can't wait very long."

He bent over the chimney and blew out the lamp. "Fine with me."

16

A pink dawn's first light was the signal to hurry. Attempting to mount, Rosa moaned about her head hurting when Slocum gave her padded butt a hard boost into the saddle. "Going to be a long day," he said.

"Being rich is not fun," she moaned.

"Oh, it will be. Take the mare's lead and start out into the street with them. Meia can drive them. I'm coming. Come on, girls, let's go!"

He was slapping butts and missing getting kicked by the honking mules as he waved them out the gate. Nodding to Meia when she passed him on her horse, he waved to Porter up on the balcony. "*Gracias, amigo,* as always."

"No, come back and bring those crazy women. I love them," Porter shouted.

"We may do that."

"God be with you, my friend."

Slocum swung in the saddle and spun the horse around and with its hooves clapping on the cobblestones, he stood in the stirrups to catch up with the women. Milk goats bleating like spooked ghosts darted around with passage of the mule train. With village women cussing them and chickens half flying for their lives and losing their feathers, Slocum and his party left the village in a hurry.

Once out in the desert, they trotted westward, stirring up dust that rose high in the sky. He wanted speed and to get there in one piece.

Gordo's Well would be their midday point, and then the well-watered mules might make Dolgres by midnight. He looked across the rolling greasewood that was knee high on his horse and saw nothing out of order—but they needed to move and be quick.

Everyone was pulling their load as he rode like a scout, searching for high places from which to look for any sign of pursuit from the village behind them. No one to trust in Mexico. These were desperate times in a land full of cactus spines and rattlesnakes, and two-legged snakes as well.

They reached the well by midday. Rosa dropped heavily out of the saddle, swept the straw sombrero off her head, staggered toward the well, and stuck her face down in the tank between two mules sucking water. At last, she rose sputtering, and spooked one mule backward with the way she looked.

"Dumbsumbitch," she cussed at him with a mad frown. "I'll give you something that damn sure will booger you."

Slocum sat his horse while they watered, rested a rifle across his lap, and was studying everyone and everything in sight. Mostly, women washing clothes on the far side. A few kids looking on at the excitement in their village, and snickering with each other at Rosa's antics. The mules did, too. Hee-haw.

A thin hard-faced woman came out of a nearby jacal. She swept the straight black hair back from her dark eyes, and told Slocum he owed her two pesos for watering his pack train, horses, and the two women. He stuck the Winchester in the scabbard and dismounted.

"Where's Gordo?" he asked her with a grin.

"Taking a siesta."

"He have a new wife?" He knew the man's habit of

rounding up some young girl to be his housekeeper and when he grew tired of her, then selling her into the *puta* trade.

"I am his wife." She stiffened her back in insult.

He paid her and she nodded sharply. "What are *you* doing with two wives?"

"One for morning. One for night." After her scowling look at him, he chuckled.

"How long can we rest?" Rosa asked, sitting on a keg with her knees spread apart and her elbows planted on them to support her chin.

"A short while."

"Good."

He led his horse over and let him drink.

Meia soon rejoined them. "We safe here?"

"Not for long. But I plan to sleep in Dolgres tonight."

Rosa used a hand to shade her eyes from the high sun to look up at him. "Good. I can sleep for days."

"Yes, we can all get some rest when we get there." He went through the animals checking girths, and satisfied, washed his hands in the tank and took some jerky Meia passed out to them. Rosa refilled their canteens from the spout while he pumped. Chewing on their jerky, they made short work of that job.

Rosa started to remount. She looked around. "Who lives here?"

"Gordo and his kinfolks." He gave her butt a one-handed shove, and she was in the saddle. The lead mare's rope in hand, she started out with a grim scowl. "Glad I don't have to live here."

"Me, too," he said over the mules' raspy protests. They didn't want to go.

With the tail of the reata in her hand, Meia moved in to slap the dull ones on the butt. Then they were on the road again, and Slocum felt easier. This would have been a sure spot for them to have to stop and an easy place for outlaws to rob them—if the outlaws knew about the ore, and by now the news of a valuable load of some kind was everywhere on their back trail. Moving as hard as they were, it would not be easy to overtake them.

He hoped so anyway, short-loping the horse ahead so that he and the women stayed that way—out in front. His stomach felt tight over the fact that he had only two women for his guards. Having several tough experienced men would be different.

Late afternoon, they entered a small village and began to water their stock at the central well. The girls ran off to relieve themselves. Slocum removed his hat and wiped his gritty wet forehead on his sleeve. As the mules and horses slurped water, he was distracted for a moment.

"Put your hands in the air, Señor," a man behind a six-gun ordered.

"Who are you" Slocum asked, slowly obeying him and wondering where the women were at.

"My name is Reynaldo and I am taking over this pack train."

"Ain't worth much," Slocum said. "Sure ain't worth dying over some panniers full of guano."

"Guano?" The man blinked in disbelief.

"Yeah, bat shit."

He made a repulsive face. "Who would want it?"

"A rich man in Guaymas for his violets."

Reynaldo looked undecided as he held the pistol on him. "I will see for myself—"

A shot rang out and Reynaldo's knees wilted. Shot in the temple, he fell to the ground. To Slocum's right ten yards away, standing behind the smoking barrel of her .44, Rosa looked hard in the man's direction, ready to shoot again.

"Who is he?" she asked, stabbing her weapon at her holster as she hurried over.

Slocum picked up the man's gun and jerked off his gun belt. They might need it. "Name's Reynaldo. He wanted our load of bat manure."

He rebuckled the belt and slung it over his horn. Meia

was coming on the run. "I heard a shot. Good way to get unconstipated."

"Rosa shot this man who was trying to steal our bat manure."

Meia frowned and obeyed his nod to mount up. Pushing her horse in close to her, Rosa said in a stage whisper, "He wants everyone here to believe we only have bat shit on them mules for some guy in Guaymas who grows violets."

"Makes sense," Meia agreed, and they left the village and the dead man lying there. Back in the desert again, the heat of the day rose to over a hundred degrees. Distant purple sawtooth ranges shimmered behind the heat waves. Mules, horses, and people were doing fine, but Slocum would squeeze every bit of strength out of them before they reached Dolgres.

"Was he alone?" Rosa asked as Slocum rode up beside her.

"I guess he was. I saw no one else. He thought, with only two women, he could take me."

"He won't get another chance either. Sorry I shot him."

"Why? He'd've killed me and raped you otherwise."

She made a pained face. "I knew it was you or him. I'd much rather you raped me than him."

They both chuckled.

The mules grew harder and harder to keep in a fast trot as the day lengthened. Their horses even grew lethargic, and needed constant booting. The closer the sun came to the western mountaintops, the more persistently their heels and spurs punished the animals they rode to make them trot.

He replaced Meia at whipping the mules to keep them going. She thanked him and rubbed her right arm, no doubt stiff from the hard effort she'd made to keep them going.

"How much farther?" Rosa asked over her shoulder.

"Couple of hours."

"Good."

*　*　*

The stars came out and the moon rose. They forded a shallow river and went up the bank into a town lit with Chinese lanterns. Fandango music filled the night, and a few party-goers turned to stare at the pack train. Slocum kept his rifle over his lap in case—he felt some relieved as they rode up the dark streets toward McNeal's compound.

An armed guard stopped them at the gate.

"Tell them Slocum is here."

The man nodded and went to the gate. "Slocum is here."

"We know of no one by that name."

"Tell Señor McNeal who is here," Slocum said, getting edgy about being in this dark street and so vulnerable.

"He has company."

"Tell him he has more."

"The *patrón* does not like to be disturbed."

"He will."

They waited.

"Will he let us in?" Rosa whispered.

"He will." Slocum wet his sun-cracked lips for the hundredth time. What was taking so long?

"Señor?" someone called down.

"Yes."

"The house help will not let us disturb him."

"I will then." He drew the extra .44 hanging on the saddle horn and emptied it in to the sky. "Now tell him Slocum is out here."

In a few minutes, a familiar voice shouted out. "Open the gate for my amigo. Slocum, sorry, they did not know who you were."

"That's fine. My gun needed to be reloaded anyway."

"Who is with you?" the man in the white suit shouted down to him from the balcony as they rode inside the yard. Hooves clattered on the brick paving.

"Two lovely rich ladies."

"Oh, how wonderful."

"You may need to guard the cargo we brought."

"*No problema.* Louis, put his panniers under lock."

"*Sí, patrón.*"

The yard bustled with stable people taking over the mules and horses. Satisfied they could handle the matter, Slocum herded his women toward the front door. A gracious straight-backed woman met them.

"I am Clarisa."

"This is Meia and this is Rosa, Clarisa. They are very rich and have been through hell to get here."

"Come with me, my dears. I have baths and even dresses to fit you." She turned to Slocum. "The *patrón* is on the second floor talking business, but he said to send you up."

"I can find my own way."

"Good. Come, ladies."

He went up the spacious staircase, his soles gritty on the smooth polished wood. McNeal came out to greet him. "It's been so long, *mi amigo,* even my help has forgotten your name. Come meet these men."

"Señor Valdez and Señor Salado, meet Señor Slocum."

Valdez was short and fat. Salado was definitely Spanish and stood erect, with his shoulders back, and gave a rather snooty look at Slocum.

"What brings you here?" asked McNeal.

"These two ladies have a mine with gold in it. One's husband was murdered over the mine, and she joined forces with the other woman."

"You've seen the mine?"

"Yes. Rich high-grade vein. They need to hire several tough, honest men to guard it, as well as workers for their mine so the gold can be extracted,"

McNeal nodded as if that was no problem.

"How rich is this mine?" Salado asked. "I might be interested in sending in one of my teams to work it on shares for them."

"I'm not an engineer or assayer, but the gold vein is impressive."

"Do they have the money to develop it?"

"Yes, we found it."

"Found it?"

"Take my word, they have enough money to develop any mine. In the Sierra Madres, Mexico, the problem is keeping it."

Valdez laughed and raised his glass. "You hit the nail on the head, *mi amigo.* Keeping it is the hard part. Here is to their health."

Slocum was not ready for the women's entrance. Both wore expensive dresses and their hair was done up. He wasn't sure they were the same two who'd ridden in there with him.

"Gentlemen, here are the mine owners. Meia and Rosa." Slocum lifted his glass to them and smiled.

All three men went around, kissed the backs of the women's hands, and bowed as they gave the women their names. Slocum went for a refill of his glass of whiskey at the bar. This would be interesting. The women's chatter soon filled the room. McNeal came over and joined him.

"Are they really rich?"

"The gold in those panniers is maybe worth half a million."

"Raw gold?"

"No, they're ingots of gold under rich ore from some mine. An outlaw named Arturo stole it, and no doubt, as usual, killed everyone there. The women became the heirs when Arturo died."

"What is your part in this?"

"I have to get back to the Madres and try to find a white woman that some Apache subchief kidnapped and brought down here."

McNeal shook his head. "With Arturo dead, the gold is really yours."

"No, it is their treasure. They can pay for their own protection. I want you to provide what they need and take care of them. Her husband's gold mine is real. I was inside it."

"When will you leave?"

"Sunup. I need to get back and I need two tough horses

to relay me back up there. You take care of my women. I trust you."

"They looked like simple village women when you brought them."

"They aren't. And there's few men in Mexico I'd trust them with besides you."

McNeal nodded at his words. "I'll take good care of them for you. Your fresh horses will be saddled before sunup. A servant will awaken you. What will I tell them?"

"I said *vaya con Dios* and for them to listen to you."

McNeal shook his head in mild disbelief. "Someday, amigo, you will get your reward."

"I have, night after night." They both laughed.

17

Mrs. Ramsey had given up on Ojo ever finding her. Rumors persisted the *federales* had killed a great Apache chief and the tribe was defeated. Only a few remaining tribesmen were left scattered in the mountains. She mended clothing for the miners, which they appreciated, and wondered how she would ever get back to the United States. Perhaps a passing Yacqui would take her. Of course, she had no money or wealth to pay them.

These hardworking dusty *indios* were always polite and very gentle toward her, thanking her for her efforts on their clothing and always holding her in some esteem at their meals, as if they were grateful she was with them. But it still did not make her any more satisfied to stay there— except she knew that the mountains without supplies and a guide would be fatal for her. Even living among the Yacqui would be much better than that.

Horses were coming off the mountain. The cook and the leader grabbed their rifles. They told her to go behind the camp and hide in case they were *federales* or *bandidos*. She set aside her sewing and obeyed them, quickly finding a place to conceal herself in the boulders at the base of a high cliff. Her heart beat hard under her breastbone and at her throat. Was this the day for her to die?

Time passed slowly, but there were no shots or sounds of an attack. Seated in her wedge with her knees at her chin, she almost regretted leaving her wood-frame house and letting the overzealous needs of her body rule her judgment. She waved away a pestering fly. *Not now. You can buzz my whole body when I am dead.*

Who were the visitors? No one came to look for her and tell her there was no danger. It was not like these people. Despite the coolness of the morning, perspiration dripped from under her arms and the hatband of the straw hat on her head.

Then the sound of a voice chilled her. "Come, woman, we must go now."

It was Ojo. She rose and saw him coming uphill for her. He wasn't dead. His bronze chest gleamed in the sunlight. Oh, thank God.

Tears welled up and ran down her face. She ran to hug his hard form. "I thought—they'd killed you."

"No, we killed them. But I had others to see about and that took longer."

"No, no worry, these people were kind to me."

"They want their land back, too, like the Dineh."

"Yes. Where will we go?"

"To my camp."

"Good." She squeezed him hard and then straightened.

"It is good." He smiled for her. "My bed has never been so empty."

She left her amigos. One old man even gave her a hand-carved cross to hang around her neck on a leather thong, and thanked her before she rode out.

"They were kind to me," she said, riding the horse he had brought her and leading the one she rode in on.

"They thought you were someone else."

"Who?"

"They are Catholics, but for many years they had no

priests, so they have their own ways of doing religion. They had never seen a white woman before. They thought you were sent to them and you were the Virgin Mary."

Mrs. Ramsey blinked her eyes. *Me? The Virgin Mary?* Oh, no, far from it. She booted her horse. This night, she'd sure lose any virginity she had achieved among them. But filled with excitement for the first time in a long time, she looked forward to that happening.

Dolgres still slept when the two women hugged him good-bye. Somehow, they'd learned of his early departure, and had no plans to let him leave without holding and kissing them.

"You will come back and check on us?" Meia asked.

"We could have more trouble, too." Rosa clung to his arm.

"All right. I'll be back after I have her in safe hands or know where they planted her."

Rosa poked him in the stomach. "And be quick about it." They all laughed as he mounted, both girls pushing his butt in the saddle.

Slocum reined the quick-footed, smoky gray barb horse down though the dark streets, leading the mane-shaking rusty red gelding beside him. These were the horses that the Moors had bred and brought from the African desert to Spain. Both were saddled and ready when he finished a hasty breakfast and left the two women waving good-bye. He'd left them in good hands.

They'd be all right. McNeal would steer them into a new society, look after their riches, and help them successfully develop their gold mine. A long way from Meia selling food on the street, or Rosa lying on her back in a house of ill repute. He hoped they would finance Grandmother's house for unfortunate women as well.

With one of McNeal's fine horses between his knees, and the second one beside him, he forded the shallow river. He was riding an animal too good for him and his needs, but it was a generous gift from his rich friend. He looked back at the village. *God go with you girls and may you enjoy your good fortune.* He let Gray run.

By late afternoon, he rode into a small village located south of the last trail he took bringing them out. Not wanting to duplicate his last route going back into the mountains, he'd chosen another way. The church doors in the village were open and he could hear singing. What day was it? No matter. He watered his horses at the community well and tank. His legs were stiff, and he stretched his arms over his head to loosen the tight back muscles.

There were hot springs around there someplace. But first, he must find some food and also feed the horses. These were not mountain mustangs, but he had made great time on them, and was grateful as he hitched them and went to see about both his and their supper.

A wrinkled-faced old woman squatting at the side of the street made him tortillas on a small grill and filled them with frijoles and peppers, rolling them up into burritos. He paid her two centavos for them.

"Too much," she said, trying to give him back one.

"No, I need information. Where can I get grain for my horses?"

"At the store." She waved behind her. "Easy to find."

"The hot springs?"

"One kilometer on the road to the mother mountains."

He paused before taking a bite. "Are there any *bandidos* close by?"

She smiled at him knowingly and then put her thin hand on his arm. "There are always *bandidos* in Mexico. This place is no exception."

"Have you heard of any Apaches?"

"*Sí.* Only a few days ago, they killed several soldiers and sent the rest back to their camp at the base."

"Is their camp close by?"

"*Sí,* maybe four kilometers up the road."

"Gracias," he said, and began to eat his supper.

"What do you need of the soldiers?"

"Mostly talk. I search for a woman taken captive in the States."

"You think she is still alive?"

"I need to know." Busy chewing his food, he waited for her answer. Sometimes, these old women could see into another world and forecast the future.

Slowly, her head bobbed. "She is still alive. But she does not wish to be rescued."

He furrowed his brow at her words and stopped eating his spicy food. "You saw her?"

"Yes."

"What was she doing?"

"A big powerful man was on top of her." The woman giggled, and then she made a circle with her thumb and forefinger. Held it up in front of his face, and she ran her other index finger in and out to show him what they were doing.

As he'd suspected, he'd talked to a bruja. Mrs. Ramsey was alive and well. How could he find her? He'd have to try regardless. In the morning, he'd go and talk to the *federales*.

That might be good or bad. Maybe they knew where he could find her, and Mrs. Ramsey could tell him herself that she didn't want to leave. He thought about that day when he'd helped her close the door against the wind. She acted like an easy woman to arouse, but like a large fire, those kind were the hardest to satisfy. Tom Horn had sounded impressed when Slocum mentioned her name. All the officers acted the same way.

Maybe they'd all sampled her. Plural wives came in all shapes and sizes. He'd known some cold as an iceberg, and others who would jump into bed at a snap of a man's finger. On the railroad coming down from Montana—he could recall Mrs. Bancock, who lived in the Big Horns. A saucy little woman in her thirties who ran a small ranch and kept rebranded stolen stock until they healed and then were driven down to Utah, where no questions were asked.

Mrs. Bancock could go on arching her back and pushing her snatch at a man for hours, screwing him if he had the stamina to do it. The secret was to get her hot enough that she came before you did. What a hellcat in bed. She'd scratch her partner's back up like he'd messed with a mountain lion. Freckle-faced, green eyes and red hair, she stood under five feet tall. She could swing up in the saddle one-handed without a stirrup, and laugh out loud at anyone who took more than one bounce to get aboard his horse.

Slocum thanked the old woman, who at the last moment reached out and stopped him from rising with her age-scarred hand. "Be careful, my son. There is much danger for you up there."

"Gracias."

She nodded and crossed herself.

The hot springs steamed in the sunset's red light when he approached them. Dismounted, he hitched the horses, and then hung the feed bags on their heads that contained corn for them to eat. He removed his hat and swept his forehead on his sleeve.

A woman rose to her feet. She was more Indian than Spanish and had a sharp chiseled face. Slender-hipped, she slinked over to where he'd tied his animals.

"You wish to take a bath, Señor?"

"Yes."

"For ten centavos, I will scrub your back and dry you with my towels." She motioned to some that were no doubt drying on the bushes.

"Good enough."

She forced a smile over her straight white teeth. "Come this way. The water is too hot here. My name is Tee-yah."

"Slocum's mine."

Then she nodded, half bowed, and thanked him as they walked down the path. "Here is the best pool."

He toed off his boots, undid his buckle, and wrapped the

ammunition belt around the holster. His gun set aside, he saw her squatted down in the twilight, not looking at him. At last undressed, he slipped into the water. The water was even hot down here. Plenty hot. She quickly shed her skirt and, naked from the waist down, followed him into the basin.

"See, I told you it was hot," she said.

Settled down on the smooth rock bottom, he agreed with her, and began to rub the hot sulfur-smelling water over his arms and upper body. Heat began to loosen his tight muscles and relax him. She washed his back with a long-handled brush and when finished, she leaned over so he could see the V between her tubelike breasts in the wet blouse. "Do you wish to soak awhile?"

He nodded.

"Fine," she said, and dropped to her butt in the water beside him. Soon, her pointed nipples showed through the thin cloth. She stirred the water with her arms and acted disinterested.

He heard one of the horses make a sharp sound. Someone or thing was messing with his horses. He rushed over, sweeping up his six-gun on the run. Water dripping off him, he drew down on the man trying to mount Gray. Slocum aimed at a spot between the rustler's shoulder blades and shot.

The man pitched headfirst off the horse, and it shied backward from him. Slocum rushed over and caught the reins. The woman came up the rise, holding her skirt against her crotch to cover her nakedness.

"Who is he?" he demanded, pointing the smoking pistol at the man on the ground.

"Montego."

"He live here?"

She shrugged. "Sometimes."

"He was stealing my horses."

"What is that? They do it all the time around here." Warily looking about in case anyone would see her dressing, she stepped into her skirt and wiggled it up her legs to cover her bare ass. Her skirt on at last, she straightened. "You are lucky. You stopped him."

By then, Slocum was dry. He rehitched the horses and went for his clothing. Still seething over someone trying to steal his horses, he shook as he dressed.

"You need a place to sleep tonight?" she asked, standing on the road above him.

"No." He didn't trust her or anyone else in this place. Somewhere beyond the stinging hot springs, he'd bed down by himself.

She shrugged in the twilight, and was gone when he glanced again in her direction. He buckled on his gun belt last. Those horses were too damn good for his kind of business. They'd be a magnet anywhere he went for men like the one he'd shot trying to steal them. Still, they were all he had, and he'd sure need both of them when he found Mrs. Ramsey.

He rode eastward under the stars. This had been an ill-fated adventure from the start, but the loss of his Apache scout, Naco, had certainly derailed his efforts after Arturo showed up, killed Naco, and left him for dead. Perhaps he should simply go back to Fort Bowie and tell the general he couldn't find her—especially without an Apache scout. Crook would understand.

Chewing on his lower lip, he considered the situation— go back or stay?

18

Mrs. Ramsey carried water in a canvas bucket uphill to her wickiup. The rushing sound of the small river behind her sounded good to her ears, like the wrens flitting in the thorny brush and the soft moan of the purple doves. It was a good morning to be alive. Not much sleep the night before, but she did feel contented again. Though a bed might have been a better place to celebrate their reunion, rather than some blankets over the rocks under her back. Who cared?

The Yacquis had treated her like a princess, but it was good to be with a virile man again. Her doubts and concerns about being a "squaw" had evaporated the night before. This was the way for her.

Soon, she would have to bar him from her wickiup, for her period would start. What a waste, but she did not wish to step over his line. Women in such distress were considered unlucky for a man to have a union with or even touch. It could lead to the man's death in battle or worse things. It never bothered her husband, nor did he have any problems doing it then. But Apaches had a different religion. The Mormons never drank coffee or tea—Indians did if they had any. Especially if they had sugar to go in it.

Ojo was gone this morning to search for signs of any more *federales* coming into the mountains. They had many supplies from the last battle, like sugar, tea, cocoa, coffee, cornmeal, flour, lard, baking powder, and salt. There was even lots of cinnamon. She loved the smell of it, and she even used it as perfume. The supplies were divided among all the women who were scattered about the hillside.

Some of the women were busy digging century plant roots to make *tiswin,* a beer made from the fermented roots. She could hear them chopping and digging in the gravelly ground uphill from her, their voices carrying down the canyon. Yellow Deer, who spoke some English and Spanish, would come by in the late afternoon and tell her all about the day's harvest.

If she had a *horno* here, she'd bake him some sweetbread. The oven at her house was Spanish style, and built by a craftsman right outside her back door. It looked like a giant beehive. She built a fire in it, let it superheat the oven, then raked out the coals and slid her loaves in with a wooden spatula. Closed the door and in an hour or so, she had golden brown bread.

She stretched her arms over her head in the fringed buckskin shirt. Maybe she could squeeze in one more wild night with Ojo before her period began. If only her system would wait that long. A prayer wouldn't hurt.

Slocum found himself deep in the Madres by the next evening. He'd located the camp setup of McCory before dark. That belligerent man's roaring voice carried in the canyon as Slocum slipped closer on foot, eyeing the camp through his brass telescope. Only reason McCory and his men were there was to waylay a pack train of gold coming out. Ike Clanton did not waste time speculating—he paid spies to send him word of such shipments, and paid them well if the robbery was a success. Like horse stealing, snitching on ore shipments was a way of life in the mountains.

Through his glasses, he saw a few white men and a hand-

ful of Mexicans in the camp. Not counting his cook and
helper, McCory had only three or four gunhands. A much
larger bunch than that, and supplies would be a nightmare
for the outlaw chief to manage. Earlier, they must have shot
a deer, and they were dressing it hanging from a cross-arm
they made. Limbs on the pines were too high to use.

Who were they after? Should he try to slip around them
and warn the pack train that was coming? By himself, he'd
have a hard time busting up McCory's camp. Maybe if he
circled the camp, he might save the pack train from an am-
bush and find some allies to help him shut down McCory's
operation for good. No telling.

He collapsed his scope, and then went back over the
mountain to where his horses were hitched. Mounting
Rusty, he led Gray, and started around the basin where
McCory was camped. To do this meant riding all night, and
he still might not intercept the intended train. The way
proved tough with only starlight, and he was forced to
make several backtracks, but by dawn he was again on the
main trail, and hoped he could find the train.

First, he heard the mules braying and saw the rifle-toting
scout out front of the train. He held up his hand as a peace
sign, and the head rider looked suspiciously at him. Then
the man began searching the forest on both sides for any
sign of an attack.

"Good day, amigo," Slocum said.

"Buenos dias."

"Ike Clanton's man McCory is camped north of here.
He's waiting for you and your cargo."

"Ay, caramba," the man said in disgust, and raised his
hand to stop the train coming up behind him. Four armed
men rode forward.

"I am Antonio Juarez," he said to Slocum. "Why, may I
ask, do you warn me?"

"'Cause I don't like McCory or Ike Clanton. Slocum's
my name."

"Both are *bastardos*, I agree." Juarez turned in the saddle and looked at his men. "Señor Slocum says that ahead, McCory who works for Ike Clanton waits for us. Chee, you go scout them out. The rest of us will take a break and decide how to fight or avoid them."

His most Indian-looking man rode off to find McCory.

Juarez turned to Slocum. "He's a good one to send. He may find a way around them."

Slocum agreed.

"Why are you in these mountains, Señor?"

"I am looking for a woman the Apaches kidnapped."

Juarez blinked in disbelief at his words. "You are a brave man, Señor."

"Or dumb."

Juarez smiled. "This woman, she is yours?"

"No. A man hired me to find her. I started with an Apache scout, but a bandit named Arturo killed him."

"Arturo is a bad man."

"No, he is a dead man."

Juarez laughed. "Listen, hombres, this man killed Arturo the *bandido*."

"You killed that sumbitch?" A big burly man rode up and looked at him in wonderment.

"Deader than a dog."

The man reached out to shake his hand. "I want to congratulate you on what you have done. There are many of us hated him for killing our relatives and friends. He was the worst *bandido* in the mother mountains. What Indian do you look for?"

"Ojo Nevado."

"Oh, you don't find small enemies to take on huh, amigo?"

Slocum smiled back at him. "No small ones."

The man shook his head in disbelief. "Slocum, you are a tough man. I'm so glad to meet you before you die." Then he laughed. "In a whorehouse at age one hundred two."

Juarez shared some jerky with him, and they all sat on

the ground waiting for the return of the scout. Rifles across their laps, Juarez's men talked, impressed with Slocum's fine horses, and then they joked about one of the guard's girlfriends and how bad she farted when he really got after her ass.

"She sounded like a Gatling gun," one man teased. "Whew, the smell was so bad, I had to go outside."

"No beans tonight, Consuela. No beans for you, girl."

"Not ever again should she eat beans, Waco."

Waco shrugged and smiled big. "But her pussy is so tight."

"Her asshole sure ain't." They all laughed.

Chee returned. He dropped off his horse lightly on his moccasin soles. He came over to where his boss rose to greet him.

"They are there all right, Juarez. They were all in camp waiting for us to ride up like he said."

"Can you shoot arrows?" Slocum asked.

Chee frowned at him. "Sure, but I don't have a bow or the arrows."

"Can you make them today?"

"Sure. Why?"

"I have some blasting sticks in my saddlebags. We can launch them into his camp like I did in Arturo's. We can run McCory off or kill him."

Juarez frowned at him. "How did you think of that?"

"Artillery in the war."

"Sí, but with a bow and arrow?"

"They land right in their lap."

Chee told the others what plants made the best arrows, and said they should get many. He went off to find a bow. The camp bustled with activity. By dark, he had six arrows and a fine bow ready to string.

The blasting sticks were cut in half, fused, and the cord was attached. Some were to be tossed in from the far side by the best throwers. The others were to arrive by arrows. The men acted excited getting them ready.

In the late afternoon, many took long naps. It was soon time for the moon to rise and them to ride over and surprise the holdup men. Slocum was impressed with the men who rode with Juarez. They were quick on their feet and hard workers.

When Slocum and Juarez approached, McCory's campfire glowed in the center of the meadow. Chee crept in closer and came back. "They are all in camp. No guards."

The plans were set. The ones going around to the far side were given plenty of time. Then, a small torch was made to light the fuses, and the bow began sending half sticks of explosive into the camp. Juarez's men were on all four sides, and the blasts threw the outlaws out of their bedrolls screaming.

"Now, let's take them, men!" McCory shouted.

Many shots were fired, and not another command came from McCory. One outlaw tried to run past Slocum. He clouted him over the head with his gun butt. The man went down like a poled steer.

In a few minutes, it was all over and they began to drag up the dead and the few alive ones to the firelight. Thick gun smoke hung in the still night air, and so did lots of the dust raised by the blasts. Slocum and Juarez searched for McCory, but he was the only one that remained unaccounted for.

"He must have got away," Juarez finally said in disgust. "I hate that the worst of all. He will come back with a vengeance."

Slocum agreed. A rat like that escaped, and you'd have him back with more of his fellow rodents the next time.

Juarez shook Slocum's hand. "We could never have done this without you. You are entitled to half the loot here."

Slocum shook his head. "Your men can use what it will

bring. His mules, horses, saddles, guns, and gear should sell at a high price."

"*Gracias,* the men will appreciate you. Are you leaving tonight?"

"At first light."

"I can ever help you, *mi amigo,* call on me."

"I will. You have fine men. Good luck to you and them." Then he went and found his bedroll. He knew that Juarez's men would do some celebrating. He'd save his for later.

Next morning, the cook served him coffee in the pre-dawn. He also made Slocum a bean burrito to take with him.

"You aren't staying for the execution this morning?" the cook asked.

Slocum shook his head. Juarez intended to execute the live ones. It was a way of life—no law—no jail—turning them loose only meant they'd prey on you again. For his part, he'd seen enough men dying in his life.

Where and how far had McCory gone? Like a wounded mountain lion, he'd be as dangerous as Arturo had been, and that jasper had nearly cost Slocum his life. Slocum rode up through the pines listening to the Mexican mockingbirds imitating a half dozen other calls. How was Mrs. Ramsey doing? Damn, where was she?

19

Isolated in the small wickiup by herself, Mrs. Ramsey shared her meadow with three deer that morning. Two does and a fawn—they acted impatient. The lead doe stomped her front hoof and kept testing the air with her long nose. She must smell something not defined enough to make her take flight. Her long ears turned in different directions to detect any sound. The deer continued to graze. Mrs. Ramsey felt privileged to be able to sit and watch them.

Two more days and she would go bathe in the river and then return to her man. It was wasted time being apart from him, but she could wait and sew her clothing. He had brought her two deer hides to make a special dress. She had no idea on what occasion she would wear this outfit. Still, she sewed the seams with care. The leather, though soft, was hard to push a needle through, and after two days, each stitch pained her fingers. But she knew he would be proud of her in it.

The deer spooked, and then the gruff voice cut the air. "You ain't no gawdamn Apache. Hell, you're a white woman."

In shock, she looked up at the man's half-blackened face.

No, he was a white man and something had caused the black part. Large and burly, he squatted down too close to her.

"What's your name, girl?"

"I am wife of Ojo Nevado."

"Bullshit, you're white. What's your name?"

"When my husband returns—"

"He ain't coming." McCory chuckled to himself. "You're on the rag. That's why you're up here."

"If you even lay a hand on me—" She wanted the buckskin out of her lap and a knife in her hand rather than the needle. She'd kill this sweat-stinking intruder.

"Where did he find you?"

She'd not answer him.

"You must be an army officer's wife. I seen you somewhere. Good, I'll save you and take you out of here."

She shook her head.

"You're afraid he'll catch you again and punish you, huh? Well, he ain't catching me. Get your things and come on." He rose and looked around. "Come on, or I'll take you along by a handful of hair. My name's McCory and I had a run-in with some outlaws last night. They didn't get me either." He reached down, grasped her arm, and jerked her to her feet. "Time for us to go."

Her heart stopped. It would do no good to scream for help. No man would come to her aid. But Ojo would find her. He would save her. He'd found her once miles away with the Yacquis. *Oh, dear God, save me from this stinking bear.*

By mid-morning, Slocum knew he drew close to the Rio Blanco. The Apaches in the past had camped along this stream. Besides its isolation, there was lots of game, especially deer, in the area.

The trail grew narrower. Timber became thicker, until Slocum came to an open meadow. Before riding in, he scanned the open space with his scope for any sign. His eye caught an image of a wickiup under a stained canvas cloth cover, and a man. Slocum could only see part of his hat, but it was one he recognized. He followed him in his scope. McCory—he shoved an Indian woman ahead of him. Dressed in buckskin, she must be a squaw—no, it was Mrs. Ramsey. He recognized her.

He was right in the heart of Apache country. If she was there, so were they. No foolish gunplay here, or he could have a mess of them down on him. Then he saw the blackened side of McCory's face. Must have gotten too close to an explosion the night before.

How did he find her? Stumbling around, no doubt. What would McCory try next with her? Getting her out of this outlaw's hands up here would not be easy. And obviously, her Apache captor wouldn't let McCory take her when he learned what had happened. So Ojo Nevado would sure be following them to get her back. So if Slocum followed them, it would only put him in the path of her Apache captor.

That left him few choices. If he followed them, he'd draw an angry Apache on his backside before the buck ever found McCory. For the moment, he'd better watch from afar until they got out of Apache country.

In a short while, he saw McCory had her riding a mule that he led. Her hands were tied and she kept looking back like she expected someone to save her. Which way would McCory go? He had to avoid Juarez and his bunch. Slocum went for his horses.

Slocum was ill prepared for making a long trek following McCory through the mountains. Somehow, he'd have to work ahead of him and check on his progress. But also, the Apache threat loomed, too. He'd have to have eyes in the back of his head most of the time. Damn, he missed Naco.

He swung wide, pressing Gray to hurry and leading Rusty. If he could get her away from McCory, he'd have the horseflesh to carry them to some safe place. The problem would be how to intercede and not get her hurt. What would a rescue be worth if she lost her life?

If McCory went out of the mountains to get as far from the Apaches as fast as possible, he'd take Valdez Canyon. Mule people hated the fast descent, but many pack trains came up it. It might be the way that McCory might try to use to exit the mountains. Slocum would have to take a chance that McCory was headed that way.

Two hours later, scrambling underneath him, Gray did a good job, but in the loose gravel, it was hard even for sure-footed horses on the steep pathway. In places, if one slipped off, Slocum would need eagle wings to float down.

The sun grew hotter by the hour, and he finally reached the canyon carved of red sandstone. From there on, the sandy wash made a better place to ride, though the temperature grew more intense and bore right down on him. Less than a few miles from the outlet, he heard disturbing sounds of someone coming up the trail. The man under a peaked straw sombrero, riding a burro and leading three more, soon came into view.

"Buenos dias, señor." He removed his hat and held it.

"The same to you."

"Such fine horses," the man said, admiring his animals. "Such a shame to use them in these badlands."

"Horses are made to use. There's a bad hombre coming behind me and he's holding an American woman hostage. Is there a side canyon back there where I can hide in until he rides by me?"

"Sí, a little ways on the left, there is a large canyon comes into this one. You could hide yourself and your horses in there."

"Gracias. This man is a killer. Avoid him."

"Oh, *gracias* to you." He crossed himself, looking relieved.

Slocum paid him two ten-centavos pieces, and the man nodded. "I will watch him closely, Señor."

The man rode on, and Slocum went in the opposite direction, until he found the side canyon and hitched the horses out of sight. Then, with his rifle in hand, he hiked back to some cover and waited. Buzzards rode the updraft, their individual shadows streaking across the wash, then on the sidewall like a living thing. He waited.

A mule brayed. The rasping hee-haw echoed in the canyon. He drew back, checked the cylinder, and then closed the lever, satisfied the chamber was full. His palm he dried on the side of his pants. He waited in the deep confines of the canyon.

Soon, the muffled sound of hooves on the sand drew closer. The black-bearded face of McCory soon showed up. He was bareheaded, standing twisted in the saddle, looking back at his back trail behind Mrs. Ramsey on the mule.

"One move and you're dead. Get your hands up!"

McCory set down his pony and raised his hands. "Why, look here, darling, we're being robbed by a real outlaw. Sumbitch, why, he ain't even wearing a mask, honey."

"Use one finger to drop that gun of yours."

"I am. I am." The six-gun hit the sand.

"Ride up a few feet and dismount. One wrong move and you're dead."

"I'm dead anyway."

"This will be a damn sight quicker."

"All right, Slocum—" He threw his right leg over the horn and dropped to the ground.

Slocum turned to the tired-looking woman. "Mrs. Ramsey, there are two horses up that side canyon. The U.S. Army sent me to find you."

"The army did what?" McCory demanded.

"They paid me to find her and bring her home."

She nodded numbly. No doubt in partial shock and bone-tired, he figured. At least she didn't refuse to go back with him—so far so good. She eased herself off the mule, and followed the directions he gave her with a head toss toward the side canyon.

"What now?" McCory asked.

"I should do like what happened to the rest of your cohorts. They were executed."

"Figured that."

"Get on your belly."

McCory acted like at first he wouldn't obey. Slocum cocked the Winchester hammer back. "I'll gut shoot you and let you die slow up here if you don't get down."

McCory obeyed him. "You know you better kill me."

"Kill yourself. I'm leaving you tied up and taking the animals. You can figure your own way home. But you better pack up and find a new country 'cause if we cross paths again, you'll be pushing up pop-eyed daisies, savvy?"

Slocum cut a rein off McCory's horse's bridle and quickly tied the outlaw's hands behind his back, then used the rest to secure one of his feet to his hands so until he got loose or someone cut him loose, he'd stay right there.

Mrs. Ramsey appeared with both horses. He led the other stock over toward her. In the saddle on Gray, he nodded at her. "Let's ride."

"Will he die there?" she asked, sounding concerned about McCory.

"I don't know and I won't miss him. Let's get out of here."

She agreed in a numb fashion, and they left McCory cursing them while lying facedown in the sand.

By evening, they were near a small village. Neither had said much all day. She rode well, only using the saddle horn for balance once in a while, and they'd made good time.

"The only bath is in this small stream." He indicated the water rushing over some rocks beside the trail. "Would you like to bathe?"

Looking bewildered, she shook her head. "Will there be other options later? I am so tired, I don't care if I'm clean or dirty."

"Yes, we'll find some. May I ask where your Apache captor is?"

"Probably following us."

Her words were so matter-of-fact, he simply nodded. If Ojo Nevado was behind them, they needed to move faster. No place would be safe short of the border.

"How did you find me?" she asked.

"I had an Apache scout. An outlaw killed him, so I was on my own after that, except I know that Nevado was somewhere on the White River by the reports I got. I was looking through my scope knowing I was close, and I spotted McCory kidnapping you."

"You saw that?"

"Yes. Lucky, I guess. Ten minutes later and I'd've missed both of you. I knew McCory's bunch had been captured by some packers the night before, so I knew he'd head out of the mountains and I guessed good. You two came along."

"I'm sorry I am not more excited about you taking me home. I'm very tired and I'm not certain I wanted to leave the Apaches."

"I should have asked you back there."

"No, it sounds rather brazen of me, but he was a good husband to me. I liked being with him. Apaches have a strange way—rules, I guess. Maybe we are strange to them, too."

Slocum agreed. They stopped for a street vendor in the dusty street, and dismounted to buy some of the old lady's food. Squatted on their haunches, they ate her spicy burritos.

"Any Apaches around here?" he asked the old woman.

"Apaches are everywhere. Like the leaves in the fall, they go and come from everywhere."

"Some around here tonight?" he asked, looking around in the twilight.

"Only some women who came to trade."

"Whose camp are they from?" she asked.

"Geronimo," the old woman said in a soft voice so no one would hear her.

Mrs. Ramsey nodded. "When did he come down here?"

"A week or so ago."

After they finished their meal, he motioned to their horses, not feeling it was safe to camp in the village, since he did not know a soul besides the old lady with her small cooker. The old woman he paid generously; then they rode out, and soon made a camp a mile from the town in a small bottom beside the creek. He unsaddled the horses and used a wet cloth to clean their backs so they didn't get galled. She wrapped herself up in a blanket despite the heat, and fell asleep on the ground.

He sat up and wondered how far away "her man" might be from them. With the two good horses rested and well watered, they could make good time across the desert. His obligation was get her back to the Arizona Territory—that would be what they did.

Two days later, without an incident, they drew near the border. The big springs on the Peralta Land Grant were barely in Arizona, but they were less than a few hours away. Neither had shared many words on the trip, and the horses they rode were now jaded. Grabbing a few hours' sleep here and there, then on the trail again. The trip had both riders depleted. Their only food was jerky and that one meal in the village.

"You can bathe at the springs. The Peraltas have enough armed guards, we can even sleep there a few hours."

"Sounds wonderful."

"I'm going to deliver you to Fort Bowie."

"That's all right. Maybe with Geronimo and the Apaches in Mexico, I can even go home."

"If that's a question, don't ask me. General Crook wanted you back."

She half smiled. "You've almost got me there."

They dropped out of the saddle at the large tank. The horses pushed in and he only let them drink a short amount, then took them back and tied them up. Too much water at one time when they were that hot, and they might founder.

When he looked up from hitching them, he could see in the twilight that she was in the water. The black and white twilight reflected on her bare skin. She waded in up to her waist, and then began to swim across the pool. Her strokes were graceful and she reached the far side, stood up, and used her hands to clear her hair back. The dark quarter-sized nipples on her pear-shaped breasts rocked back and forth in the gathering darkness.

He toed off his boots and then undressed. He stepped in the tepid water, feeling the fresher springwater feeding it as he went out farther. She swam to him and rose up to throw her arms around him, which about upset him, but he recovered.

Their mouths meshed, and she became excited for more. His hand cupped her breast—firm and wonderful under his palm.

"We can get a bed—" His words were cut off by her finger.

"Since the day you closed my back door, I have wanted you. I can do it on a blanket. We don't need anyone. Just us, you and me."

He shook his head and looked off toward the lights at the ranch across the way. Who needed them?

20

Mrs. Ramsey lay snuggled with her back against the rock-hard form of her rescuer, who was nested around her. How many times had they plunged into blazing sex the night before? The man was without pause, too. Her head felt dazed. She didn't want to go into Fort Bowie looking like that. Who cared? This would be their last night together.

She turned over, reached down, and began to pull on his wonderful root. One more time for him to stop the itching inside her vaginal walls. In minutes, he was sprawled on his back and she dropped down to straddle his stiff post.

She wished she would not have to give him up in twenty-four hours. Oh, he felt so good inside, and now he was beginning to raise his butt up to meet hers. Oh, God, please let me keep him.

Please.

Daybreak, Slocum took a quick swim, saddled their horses, and they set out for Bowie. A hard day's push, but he intended to deliver her to the general or Crook's man—whoever was there.

The day went by without incident, and by evening they were riding up into the pass.

"Will you drop by and see me some time?" she asked. "If his buggy isn't there. At times, he may be weeks getting back."

"Yes, if I get a chance."

She looked over at him. "Promise?"

"Promise."

"Good, so I can look forward to something out there."

"What if Ojo Nevado comes back for you?"

She looked off at the towering Chiricahuas. "He's not coming."

"How do you know?"

"He's never been this long before."

There was no answer for him to give her.

When they rode up in the twilight, the sun already set behind the Dragoons, Lieutenant Moates came out on the porch of the day command post. He blinked his eyes twice in disbelief. "That you, Slocum? Mrs. Ramsey? Oh, dear God, we thought you both were dead."

"Naco is dead. He was killed by some outlaws who are now in hell." Slocum dropped out of the saddle, and then he helped Mrs. Ramsey down.

He turned to Moates. "We're starving."

"Come in. Come in. Private Ward, go get them lots of food and on the double."

"Yes, sir." The soldier left, turning up dust with his boots in a hard run.

"The general is in Tucson," Moates said. "I'll wire him the news. Ma'am, are you all right?"

"Yes," she said in a dry voice.

Slocum looked over the empty-looking base. "You get permission to go into Mexico?"

"Yes, and we have Captain Crawford and Tom Horn with a party of scouts down there now. There are two companies of cavalry on the border waiting for word from them that they've located the hostiles."

Slocum and Mrs. Ramsey ate the meal delivered to the command post, and Slocum was actually full for the first time in weeks. The evening had turned into night by then, and one of the officers' wives offered Mrs. Ramsey a place at her quarters to sleep and freshen up.

Mrs. Ramsey reached over and squeezed his forearm. "Thanks for all you did for me, Slocum."

He looked up and nodded. No more words were needed. She would have a difficult time ahead adjusting back into her role as a polygamous wife, but she was a survivor. A big one. After all she'd been through, she'd come out on top. He watched her leave as she talked softly to the woman who was boarding her.

"You need a place to sleep?" Moates asked him, pouring some more of the general's good whiskey in his glass.

Slocum raised it in a toast. "Here's to Crawford's success. No, I can find a place."

"You ever see Ojo Nevado?" Moates asked.

"No. But he's down there. I don't know how he didn't find us, except we really fled the Madres when I finally found her. I took her away from one of Ike Clanton's henchmen named McCory, who'd kidnapped her away from the Apaches."

"Sounds confusing as hell to me."

"It was. But she's back and that's what the general asked for." Slocum drank some more of his great whiskey.

"Amen."

He left his horses at the stables and with a blanket roll on his shoulder, he walked down to the walnut tree in the wash below the big spring in the moonlight. He had just unfurled it when a short figure wrapped in a blanket paused over beside some catclaw and looked around. Then she looked directly in his direction.

She clutched the blanket at her throat and looked up at him. "Me Josie. You remember me?"

"I sure do, Josie."

"Good," she said, and swept off the blanket, standing

naked in the pearl starlight before him. "Let's get in your bed."

He bent over and kissed her. "I thought you'd never get here."

When he finished kissing her, she held the back of her hand to her lips like he'd burned them. "Hurry."

Just before the dawn, he slipped out of the covers and dressed. She rolled over with a soft grunt and went back to sleep. He left her his blanket roll. Small price to pay for such a sweet one to share a bed with. How she knew he was even there, he couldn't say, but Apaches knew everything.

He took mess with Moates. They sat on the benches opposite each other in the large tent, and sipped the strong fresh coffee that was waking Slocum up.

"Where will you go next?" Moates asked.

"Back to Mexico and check on some ladies that have a mine down there and see how they are faring. I met them looking for Mrs. Ramsey."

Moates shook his head. "You're a wonderment. What were you, a captain in the war?"

Slocum nodded.

"I think serving under you would have been a wild party every day."

"I'd had you with me, the South might've won the war."

They both laughed.

He left Rusty at Fort Bowie. He told the sergeant in charge of the stable if he wasn't back in a month or wrote to him about the horse, to give the horse to an Apache woman named Josie. He headed south, a little less hurried than coming in, but made the Peralta Ranch by evening.

The ranch foreman, Vega, clapped him on the arm and nodded in approval. "Your amigo Horn was through here, you know. He took the boys' money again riding some crazy horse they'd been saving for him to ride."

"He's with Captain Crawford in the Madres now."

"*Sí.* Horn and those scouts will find the Apaches. What can I do for you?"

"I need a hammock for the night and some frijoles."

"Juan, take the señor's horse and put him up and feed him. Come, we have food ready to eat."

"Gracias, amigo."

"No problem. I hope they can gather all those wild Apaches so we can ranch this place again."

"Many more wish the same thing."

"I know, I know," Vega said, and led him to the main house.

After a fine meal, a young woman showed him the hammock under a ramada where he would sleep. Ready to leave, she asked, "Is there anything else you will need?"

"No. *Gracias.*"

She curtsied for him and hurried away.

He needed shut-eye and lots of it. The trip on to Dolgres would be exhausting. Somewhere a coyote let out a yip in the growing darkness. He'd be out sleeping with them next. Better enjoy the hammock while he could.

At dawn, he left headed south. He'd bought a new thick-woven cotton blanket at the ranch store, and rolled it tight with rawhide strings for a bedroll. Some crackers, dry cheese, and jerky and he had his supplies. Two canteens on his saddle horn and the "gray ghost" as the ranch hands called his gelding—he left the main headquarters and crossed the long-deserted crop fields for the desert and its saw-toothed mountains. Years of raids and incursions by the Apaches passing back and forth over the Peralta Grant going to and from the Madres had kept the ranch out of business.

In three uneventful days, he made the crossing and arrived at McNeal's casa. McNeal was gone to Mexico City on business. The girls were in the mountains at the mine and all reports were good. He'd rest the horse for a day before heading across for the Madres. Lounging around the spacious mansion in a robe while they washed his clothing, he enjoyed the luxury of his friend's fine home. The cooks in the kitchen all teased him when he ventured in there at mealtime.

Guests were supposed to eat at the great table and be served, not pour their own coffee or eat off the working kitchen table. The cooks made him fancy desserts of fried red bananas with whiskey sauce poured over them. By evening, he was dancing with one of the maids on the tile kitchen floor while two others sang and strummed guitars. The maid's name was Yuba. Short with a nice ass and handsome face. He could whirl her like a top.

Out of breath, he finally took her by the waist and put her on the kitchen table. He kissed her, and then she drew up her skirt. He ran his palms up the outside of her smooth short shapely legs, and a chill went up his back. Soon, he discovered that she wore no underwear. Being a daredevil, she scooted to the very edge and unbuckled his pants. In seconds, they dropped to his knees. With her fierce grip on his dick, she stuffed him in her tight pussy, and then leaned back on her stiff arms to raise her butt enough for him to go deeper. He went as far in as he could go, and she pressed her body against him for more.

Her wild hair in her face, her full lower lip dropped as she sucked in air—they made love on the kitchen table. The two guitarists never stopped making wild music. He savored every moment of it, right up to the time when his gun finally went off and she gasped.

He pulled up his pants, and then he swept her up in his arms. After a tender kiss, he set her on the floor, making sure she was steady enough to stand before he let go of her. The other two applauded.

Yuba shook her head, a glow of embarrassment on her face. Then, with her palm, she slapped his muscle-corded belly under his shirt. "I loved every minute of it."

"Good, so did I."

"Next time you can play the damn guitar and I'll dance

with him," the larger of the two musicians said, and they all laughed.

Later, he stood in the second-story bedroom and listened to the night sounds coming in the open balcony door. The sun was down and it was at last beginning to cool down. A breeze swept his face. Flickering lights and city noises came on the wind. Busy place.

In the morning, he'd head for the mine. Sleep under the stars. There was a light knock on the door.

"Yes?"

"Open the door," a woman said.

He did, and in the hall light stood the buxom guitar picker with a sheepish look on her full face. "I ain't Yuba, but I can play this guitar and sing you to sleep. My name's—"

"Patricia," he said, and invited her into the room.

She swept in, looking around as if the near-dark room was a new place she'd never seen before.

"I've never been up here before. I work in the kitchen. I was afraid—"

"Afraid of what?"

"Afraid you'd send me away."

"Why would I do that?" he asked as he showed her the bed to sit upon.

"I'm not as pretty as she is."

"Can she play the guitar as well as you can?"

"To be honest—no." Busy picking a chord or two, she didn't look up at him.

"So you came upstairs afraid I'd turn you away— because you don't have a little shapely body. Go ahead, play your guitar. I never was accompanied by music before tonight just for two of us doing it."

They both laughed.

"I'm getting undressed," he said. "Do you want to?"

In the half-light, he saw her chew on her lower lip—her courage might be taking wing. Then she set the instrument on the bed and scooted to the edge. "Why not?"

"Why not?" he said, toeing off his left boot. "Can you play the guitar naked?"

With the blouse half over her head and her large plump breasts exposed, she shrugged. "I guess I can."

The blouse clear of her hair, she laughed, pulling it off her arms. "I must have sometime. Just not with—you."

He blew out the small bedside lamp and then in the semidarkness, watched her shed the skirt off her hips and push it downward. Lots of woman there. Not the petite Yuba, but certainly shapely enough to make love to.

Soon, they sat cross-legged on the deep feather bed facing each other, and he handed her the guitar. "Play us some music. It may settle your nerves down."

"Nerves?" She threw her head back and looked at the ceiling as her nimble fingers began to draw music from the strings. "I have no nerves left."

With a wary shake of her head, she began to sing softly about the "wild mustang." A Mexican ballad. Her voice, though a little husky, had an alluring ring to it, and her expertise at playing supported her voice and made him think there was an orchestra in the room.

How many nights during the war would he have paid her a million dollars to have her come and sing him this song? He was galloping with the wild steed, and the thunder of his hooves came from her fingers, as she weaved the story in song to a hard crescendo at the end.

"Don't quit."

"You like my music?"

"Of course I like your music. It's very moving." He had to get on his knees to reach her, and then he kissed her hard on the mouth.

When he sat back on his legs, she tossed her shoulder-length hair back and swallowed hard. "Oh, I could play all night for that."

"Good," he said and smiled at her. "Play some more."

The next song was a hard strumming polka like he and Yuba had danced to earlier. He rocked back and forth on his butt, responding to the inviting music. When she finished, he moved to her, set the guitar aside, and took her in his arms. She rose on her knees and pressed her hard full breasts into his chest. Soon, he was feeling her left nipple turn to stone under his palm. He was heady with a growing need, and his hand slid over the mound of her belly and his finger combed through her pubic hair.

She sucked in her breath. The moment of resistance passed and she spread her legs apart for him. In a minute or two, she was on her back as he gently probed her with his index finger and kissed her.

At last on his knees between her wide-open legs, he nosed his half-full dick in her gates. It was plenty stiff enough to ease against her ring, and then as he probed her gently—his rising erection went through the gates.

She cried out and clutched him. A nice way to be rocked to sleep—music and a woman's fine body to penetrate—he was spoiled.

21

Three soldiers drove Mrs. Ramsey back to her place. Sergeant Yancy and two privates, Calley and Holms. Holms, a young freckled-faced boy, drove the army wagon and apologized to her for every bump. Their boss and Calley rode horses and carried repeating rifles across their laps. She'd ordered fifty pounds of flour, some lard, sugar, raisins, dry apples, bacon, and some barley for her livestock from Gunner's Store in Bowie, promising him that her husband would come by and pay him. With no idea what was left at her place, she chose not to do without.

Besides, Onswell could afford it. As they crossed the Sulfur Springs Valley in the wagon, she wondered how her first meeting with him would go. Why worry? She'd lie on her back on the bed like she always did and let him "ravage" her, if one could call it that.

She'd miss Slocum. Be hard to forget him. She looked at the clear azure sky, and then the light dust that boiled up from the horses' hooves and the iron-rim wheels. Be another hot day.

Later this day, she'd be alone after these three left, and she'd get down to wearing maybe only a shift—or nothing.

Ojo must have watched her feeding her chickens wearing only a skirt in the cool morning. She would need to become more careful of what she wore and when.

How long before Onswell arrived at her place? She'd have to practice her sniffling. Where was the big silent man who brought her back to Bowie? Down in Mexico, no doubt. Would he ever come by again? She hoped so.

The next evening, Slocum arrived at Porter's large wooden gate under the flowery bougainvillea vines. His friend rushed out on the balcony and shouted to him down in the street. "Are you all right?"

"I'm fine."

"Open the gate for my amigo."

"It *is* open." Slocum waved and rode inside.

"You are all right? The Apaches didn't roast you?"

"Do I look roasted?"

"No, but they do that. The boys will put your horse up and grain him. Come on, we have much to talk about." Porter looked around, and then herded him inside. The pleasant-smiling Estela held the door open for them.

"Good evening," she said, and he knew from the tone of her voice that she was expectant.

"The women left here days ago on the way to their mine," Porter rambled on. "I like them, especially Rosa. She really knows how to party."

"Good women. I am headed up there in the morning."

"What about the woman the Apaches took hostage? Is she alive?"

"Yes, and should be back on her farm."

"You have great adventures and I piss in a pot. But, my amigo, be careful. I heard yesterday that Ike Clanton found out about you wiping out his best gang of outlaws and he's put a big price on your head."

"How much?"

"For your head in a gunnysack, one thousand dollars."

"I should sell it to him."

"Oh, don't be silly. He is a miserable excuse for a man. He rustles cattle and then he sells them to the U.S. Army and Indian agents. His men rob pack trains and kill everyone."

"I know." Slocum took the glass of whiskey and nodded to his friend. "I'll watch out for his men."

"It could be anyone. In Mexico, a man would shoot his own brother for that much money."

"I know about that. The girls were all right when they rode through here?"

"Oh, *sí*. They must be very rich now. They ordered some jewelry from me. I sold Meia some gold earrings that are big as hoops for her ears."

"I'm going up and check on them in the morning."

"Give them my love."

"Now I'm going to take a bath." Slocum nodded to Estela, standing in the doorway with a robe over her arm.

Porter nodded his approval. "Just be careful."

"With her?" Slocum tossed his head at the woman.

"Especially her."

Inside the large bathroom, he kissed her and she clung to him. In a few more moments, they were undressed, she was bent over, and he was holding her hips to steady her as he pumped his hard dick to her.

"Ahhhhh," she cried out as his belly fit hard up against her ample rump and his dick struck the very bottom. He rode her hard, and in the end came with a full throttle into her. Her knees buckled, and only him holding her saved her from falling face first into the tub. The "rest of the bath" took an hour.

He didn't see her again until early morning in the kitchen. He drank her strong coffee and ate her sweet cinnamon-raisin rolls. There were none of the other girls there that morning rushing about, and when he finished eating, she came and sat on his lap.

With her hand, she swept the hair back from his forehead and then kissed him. "See what you have been missing?"

"I won't miss it again."

"Good. I sent you some rolls to eat on the way. A lot of fresh jerky and some other things to eat today." She hugged him. "That may be silver in my hair, but I am still a woman."

"You sure are. You sure are."

They kissed, and he left for his horse, Gray, which Juan's boys had saddled and ready. He rode out of the village when the cocks began to crow. He planned to be high in the Madres by nightfall.

The fastest way in was up the front face. It was also the sheerest route. At midday, he met a pack train coming off the trail.

He paused and visited with the headman, who rode a good bulldog sorrel horse made for the Madres. Short-legged, squat, and powerfully built, the red horse was the picture of what a mountain horse's conformation should look like.

"Much traffic ahead?" he asked the man.

"I saw no one since I left the Dawes Mine. My name is Loredo."

"Slocum is mine."

The man nodded like he knew that. "I know you are the man that stopped Ike Clanton's gang."

"I let McCory go, though."

"A shame, but it will be months before he can round up enough tough cutthroats to be any threat."

"You have faced him before?"

"*Sí*, and I have lost some good men, too."

"Thanks. I better get going."

"Have a safe trip and shoot some more *bandidos*."

Slocum nodded and waved to his crew, then rode past them. It was late afternoon when he was approaching the country where the Outhouse Mine was located, and he heard shots. Like short firecrackers, they popped here and there— like a siege.

He sent the big horse forward uphill in great lurches. The sure-footed barb made great strides cat-hopping up the mountain, and at last was on top. In a long lope, Slocum crossed the flat mountaintop looking for any shooters. Then he spotted a half dozen horses hitched in the pines. He reined up and rode in amongst them, reached over, and cut their girths nearly in two. Most of the cinches would break when the riders went to get on. Then, he took Gray a hundred yards north and concealed him better. Rifle in hand, he ran to the rim, and could see the smoke from one shooter on his left halfway down the mountain. Then the hat of another showed in some bushes, and he began to see others stand up and take shots at the men concealed around the mine entrance.

He chose the one on the left and took aim. The bullet went his way. Hit hard under the arm, the raider threw his rifle in the air and pitched over head-first to roll down the hill a good ways. Slocum swung the .44/40 around, ejecting the cartridge, and took another shooter, who was looking aghast at the first in his sights. Slocum's finger squeezed off the shot. Hot lead struck the man in the side of the face and he went spilling downhill.

A cheer went up, and the men from the mine charged the hill, screaming and shouting, their guns blazing. In seconds, the other attackers threw up their hands in surrender.

He looked them over—one was missing—McCory. Slocum turned on his heel and raced toward the attackers' horses. He was there in time to see McCory had fallen off one horse, saddle and all. In the process of mounting another, McCory slapped the animal hard with his reins and shouted. The horse's burst of speed was enough to snap the last girth strings.

For a moment, when McCory and the saddle came off the rump of the horse—he actually flew through the air like a trapeze artist for a few seconds, then landed facedown, his feet hung up in the stirrups and him cussing like a blue sailor.

Beating the ground with his fists, McCory screamed, "You no good sumbitch. How did you do this to me?"

"You want me to start at the beginning?" Slocum tossed aside the man's rifle and jerked him up by the collar, half-choking him until he grew red-faced. "Listen, I told you to never get in my way again. Those women down there are my women. I don't want them bothered, you savvy?"

"Yes! Yes," McCory gasped.

Slocum threw him down and jerked the six-gun out of McCory's holster, then stuck it in his own waistband. Red-faced, Meia and Rosa came up over the hill.

"You're back!" Rosa shouted, and then drew her gun and shot twice.

Slocum turned in time to see the derringer slip from McCory's hand. His chin dropped, his legs still tangled by the stirrups, and he pitched forward and sprawled on the ground kicking and thrashing.

Slocum went to Meia and Rosa and hugged them to him. "Don't look. He's dying."

"We prayed for you to come. We prayed hard for you today. Our men are brave, but these bandits are tough killers," Rosa said, sobbing.

"We really prayed," Meia said, hugging him around the waist. "And you came. Oh, I love you, Slocum. I have missed even sharing you so much."

"How is the mine coming?" he asked, herding them in that direction down the steep hillside.

"We about have the whole caved-in entrance cleared and timbered."

"You have made good time," he said.

"Yes, very—"

Rosa planted her feet and gave a head toss behind her. "What about him?"

"We'll bury him later."

"What if he's not dead?"

"He will be before sunset."

She wrinkled her nose and they went on.

A shot went off and Meia jumped. "What was that?"

"That was called delivering them to their Maker," said Slocum.

"They are going to kill all of them?" Rosa asked, speaking in Spanish as if upset.

"Yes."

"Oh."

Meia broke in. "Did you know that the soldiers are here in the Madres to catch the Apaches? U.S. soldiers and their scouts. Captain Crawford came by and ate a meal with us. He's a very nice handsome man."

"Yes, I know him. I was at Fort Bowie a week ago and heard all about it."

"With the Apaches gone and the outlaws dead, perhaps we can run the mine—"

Slocum shook his head. "Why don't you two sell it to those friends of McNeal's and let them have all the danger here in these mountains?"

"What could we ask for it?"

"A million dollars."

"What?" Meia slapped her forehead, and then shared a head-shaking look with her partner.

"Asking and getting are two different things. But with a good lawyer, we could start there," Slocum said.

"You'd help us?"

"Find a lawyer, yes. Negotiate, no."

"Where do you need to go next?" Rosa asked.

"Over some old mountain. You girls are going to do all right."

"Yes, we have thousands of dollars in the big safe. We sent Grandmother five hundred in small coins so she can continue her work," Meia said.

"You know she'll do lots of good with that money," Rosa said to him.

"She did, and she will do more. Maybe you two'd like to take a trip around the world when you sell the mine?"

"A dumb Mexican woman and an ex-*puta*?"

"Decked out in fancy silk and satins, they will never know that. They will want your wealth to rub off on them."

Meia wrinkled her nose. "You sound so certain. How will we know how to act?"

"Hire a woman who will be your secretary, and she must have vast experience, and make her tell you what you must and must not do."

"What do you think, Rosa?"

"I say we do it."

"All right, we will do it."

"Good, that's settled."

Rosa twisted and shaded her eyes with her hand to look at the sun time. "How long till sundown? I want this man in my bed."

"In our bed," Meia insisted.

"Oh, *sí*, but we must have hours left."

"Why?" Meia asked. "We can do it any damn time we want. We're two rich bitches."

"Let's talk to your help and see how many outlaws are left alive and what we must do so they don't disturb us," Slocum said.

Rosa said, "For heaven sakes, yes, let's do that first." Then they all three laughed and clapped each other on the back. "Good job. Well done so far."

22

The news came that morning to the Outhouse Mine that Captain Crawford had been shot and killed by some Mexican irregulars during a three-way battle with the Apaches. Tom Horn had taken the captain's body to a village over west with a church and cemetery to have him interred there. It was a somber time for the troops and the scouts. Crawford was considered the most skilled at leading the Apache army scouts after their own people. In Slocum's judgment, he was the best.

"This Tom Horn is your friend?" Rosa asked Slocum over breakfast. "Does he need you?"

"Do you wish to ride over there and be with him?" Meia asked. "We and these men that McNeal hired for us can hold and work this mine. If you think you are needed, why don't you go see what you can do for him?"

Hungover from a night of making love with two hungry women, he tried to let the fresh-made hot coffee clear his head. "It might be a good idea."

The word was that Horn had taken Crawford's body to San Tomas. A small village in the foothills, like so many others down there. Slocum could reach the place with luck by afternoon. If he could comfort Horn any, the trip would be worthwhile. While he dreaded what he had to face, he saddled Gray and kissed both women good-bye, then rode off to find his friend.

The trip was long, hot, and dusty. When he arrived in San Tomas, an old man he stopped on the street told him the cowboy who earlier had brought in the body was in the Nogales Cantina. Slocum dropped out of the saddle heavily and his knees threatened to buckle. Grasping the saddle horn for a moment, he steadied himself. He looped the reins over the worn rail and then loosened the cinch.

There was music and a husky-voiced girl was singing a ballad inside. Glasses clinked and men's voices trailed outside. He stopped on the porch to allow his eyes to prepare for the darker interior. He shouldered through the swinging doors and readjusted the holster on his right hip—a move he made out of habit, which caused no eyebrows to raise.

Under the felt hat with a lock of dark hair hanging over his forehead, Tom Horn turned and saw Slocum. "Get over here."

The slur in his words told Slocum he'd been drinking for a while. "How are you?" asked Slocum. "I heard this morning over at the mine about Crawford's death and came to see if I could do anything."

"Glad you came, pard." Tom turned to the bartender. "Gustavo! Get my friend Slocum here a clean glass to drink out of."

"*Sí, señor.* Welcome to San Tomas."

Slocum nodded that he'd heard his welcome.

When the glass arrived, Horn filled it half full with good whiskey. "We got more, too."

"Anyone else come with you?" Slocum asked.

"Yeah, Lieutenant Graves. He's in the crapper out back. Got him a bad case of the shits. I mean bad."

"You need some blackberry root tea," Slocum said. "Hey, Gustavo, you got any blackberries that grow wild around here?"

"*Sí, señor.* Down on the creek there are berries growing, but they have no berries now."

"I know. I want some roots from them. Send some boys down there. I want lots of the roots. Put some water on to cook—maybe two pots or so."

"What are you making medicine for?"

"The lieutenant has the shits."

"Will it work?"

"Yes, and tell them to hurry."

Gustavo waved at him that he understood, and then he hurried to the back door, shouting for some boys to come work.

The whiskey was beginning to work on Slocum when three hard cases dressed in buckskin came through the doors and strode to the bar. Something about the hard cases and the way other men shrank away from them made Slocum suspicious.

"Who are they?" Slocum asked Gustavo under his breath when he went by.

"Scalpers. They scalp Apaches and collect the bounties."

Slocum had heard about scalpers. Only thing he knew about them was that they often lied about the black hair they brought in, which could have been from an Apache, Indian, or a Mexican. Hated and feared, they rode rough-shod over people while collecting the Mexican government's bounties on scalps.

"Hey, you Horn?" one of them asked.

"Yeah, I'm Tom Horn. What about it?"

"We been doing your job for you."

"How's that?"

"We got us a powerful Indian today. You gringos could never catch him. But we did—today."

"Who's that?" Horn asked.

"Come out here," the big man said. "I'll show you."

"Wait." Slocum tried to stop him from going outside, but Horn shrugged him off.

"They've got some evidence they want me to see." He

waved Slocum off. So instead, Slocum followed him out, growing more sober by the minute over what the situation might turn into.

"Here." The man behind the thick handlebar mustache lifted from his saddlebags a still-wet scalp. "Guess who this sumbitch is, boys."

"Who?" Horn asked with his thumbs stuck over his waistband.

"Why, he's a chief, boys. I mean, he was a chief. His name is Snow Eye."

Ojo Nevado. Her man. Was it really his hair? Who could say? These men were liars and outlaws. "You sure?" Slocum asked.

"Gawdamn right I am. We kilt that sumbitch early this morning."

"What else you got for proof?" Tom asked. He then turned to Slocum. "Ojo was a bad bastard to try and track."

Slocum agreed, and thought that the deal was a hoax.

"This," the scalper said, and produced a snowy eyeball in the dirty palm of his hand.

Tom leaned over and studied it, then looked up at the man. "I guess you did."

"Gawdamn right we did."

"Why don't you load your three asses up and leave here?" Horn asked the men standing in the middle of the dusty street.

"What the fuck for?"

"'Cause I said so. I was sick over Captain Crawford's death. I've been sick for months seeing you boys' handiwork all over. Little Injun kids and women with their throats cut by bad sons a bitches like you." Tom was getting his ire up, and he started to wade in on the scalper.

Slocum tried to stop him, but Horn shrugged off his restraint. "These no-good bastards—"

"Who're you calling a bastard?"

"You—you damn killer of little kids—load your ass up and get the hell out of here. You're making me sick. I may puke all over you."

Slocum saw the other two slip out of the cantina and stand along the wall. They would be tough no matter what. The one with the pencil-thin mustache would be the fastest he had to face. Drunk or sober, Tom could take care of the one he had backing up. But the other two he'd left for Slocum.

"All of you scalpers get the hell out of here." Horn waved his arms to drive them out. "We're having an Irish wake for Captain Crawford and the likes of you three degrade it."

A clock began ticking in Slocum's brain. It ticked slowly, but he knew that unless a divine force stepped in, in a very few minutes there'd be a shooting in the street. In the long shadows, he wished for more light. There would be less as the seconds clicked by.

"I don't know who the fuck you are, mister," the first scalper said. "But I ain't taking any of your lip."

Wrong answer.

Horn's right hand filled with his Colt and it was belching smoke, bullets, and death. Slocum's first shot slapped the man with the mustache in the chest. The bullet cut him short of drawing. The second man's pistol misfired and he took a slug in the gut. When he tried to shoot at them again from the ground, Slocum shot him in the face.

The acrid gun smoke hung in a thick cloud. Not a breath of air moved. The upset horses at the hitch rack began to settle down. Slocum moved out of the bitter fog, coughing hard and wondering if the scalpers had any allies. Finally, he holstered his six-gun and put his shoulder to the plastered wall. *Damn mess.*

"Son," Horn called to him, and soon he came over with tears streaming down his cheek. "This past week Captain Crawford and I found two small camps of women and children murdered and scalped by the likes of them bastards. We should've hung them by their feet with their heads over a hot fire and boiled their brains like the Apache do to their worst enemies." He herded Slocum back through the bat-wing doors.

"Crawford said someone needed to stop them bastards. We did it this afternoon. God bless him. Let's go drink."

Horn slapped a ten-dollar gold piece on the bar. "Here's to bury them, Gustavo. Now crack another bottle open. We're getting drunk."

Slocum saw the pale-faced lieutenant seated at a table sipping something. He and Horn walked over with fresh glasses and a new bottle. Horn set the quart down hard. "You any better?"

"I don't know. There can't be much more left in me."

"That tea will help. Drink lots of it," Slocum said.

"What the hell is it?"

"Blackberry roots. They use it in patent medicine. It works."

Horn agreed. "You drink that, we'll work on this whiskey."

"A while ago I heard shots outside?"

"Three scalpers gone to Hell," Horn said.

Graves agreed with a hard nod. "That was gruesome— what those guys did."

"They ain't killing another baby again." Horn punctuated his sentence with a fist pounding on the table.

In the morning, Slocum woke up in a hammock. His head hurt worse than if he'd been beaten up. The swinging motion made him want to throw up. He put his feet over the side and steadied things. There had been some woman undressing him the night before. All his clothes were there. Then, some rooster cut loose and shattered his thoughts. Whew, it would be a hard day. He dropped back on the hammock and held his throbbing forehead. Maybe he could simply sleep all day.

A woman brought him a tray with food and a steaming cup of coffee. He felt a little uncomfortable being naked, and pulled a blanket over his legs. She put the tray on his lap.

"The eggs are scrambled. The pork sausage is fresh and I made the tortillas."

He looked up in her face and nodded. *"Gracias."*

"Oh, it is nothing. We know that you grieve for the captain."

She was not pretty and her upper teeth stuck out when she talked. Hell, drunk and in the dark—he blew on the steam, hoping the coffee would clear his brain.

"My name is Maria if you need me."

"Who paid for this?"

"It came from a fund."

"What fund?"

"Gustavo has it. It came from the scalpers' pockets and money belts. They had lots of money on them. We will pay for things that need to be paid for from it."

"Thank everyone, it's been a helluva deal."

She agreed and left him. He watched the swing of her trim hips as she went inside the jacal. Hell, if he'd had a union with her the night before, he didn't recall it, but there were lots of them he couldn't remember. *Ah, hot coffee at last.*

Slocum left Horn at mid-morning and rode back to the Outhouse Mine. He slept some off the trail, and then arrived at the mine at sunup. Rosa ran out and hugged him.

"Bad deal?"

"Some of it. Oh, Crawford was buried in the church cemetery. All that went all right. I'll tell both of you the rest over breakfast."

His horse put up, he washed his hands in the water tank and headed for the mess tent. Stiff and sore, he ducked to enter. Sleeping on the ground those few hours the night before had hurt him. He blinked his dry eyes and ducked going inside the tent.

Meia, in an apron, nodded in approval at the sight of him. "He is back."

The men sitting around the rough tables nodded to him.

"How was the trip?" Meia asked.

"He's going to tell us at breakfast," Rosa said, swinging on his arm.

So between bites of their food, he explained about the death of Ojo Nevado and the scalpers. A woman was on each side of him vying competitively for his attention. Not bad.

He spent the next two days entertaining the two rich women—in bed. In the hammock anyway.

"You mean you won't take any of our gold or money?" Meia asked, sitting astride him as naked as Eve and holding her teacup breasts in her palms.

"I have plenty of money left. The army paid me well to find Mrs. Ramsey and bring her back."

"You think she loved him?" Rosa asked.

"I never asked. But she must have—somehow. She never complained about him. She sure did about McCory."

"Then she fell in love with him—Ojo Nevado?" Rosa frowned.

"Might have."

"Reckon she knows he's dead?"

He shook his head. "No telling."

"When are you leaving us?" Meia asked

"In the morning."

Rosa scowled in disgust. "Aw."

"You will soon be heading in with a pack train of gold."

Meia tossed her hair back. "When I'm in China or France, I'll think about you."

"Good."

"Why good?"

"You must only remember the good things and have fun."

"We will," Rosa promised him. "She's the sister I never had."

He yawned big. "I'm going to sleep a few hours."

She slapped his rock-hard belly and wiggled her butt on top of him. "Not yet."

23

Mrs. Ramsey had finished drying the last plate and stood on her toes to put it on the stack in her cabinet. Dishes done, she noted how the wind swept her new linen curtains and sunshine splashed in her kitchen. The new oilcloth table covering—she straightened the four chairs and stopped. Her kitchen looked nice. With the new coat of paint Onswell promised he'd bring her on his next trip by, she'd have the kitchen fixed up.

The damn coatimundi kept getting her new chicks. Maybe she could shoot him, but that would require using stealth and shooting well in the dark—two things she had little faith she could do.

The few pieces of small underwear she'd hand-washed that morning—she never wore the saint's undergarment unless Onswell was there. Long-handle underwear was all right for winter in Utah, but not summertime in southeast Arizona Territory. In fact, she had nothing on under the ruffle-fronted housedress she wore.

Hang these small pieces on the line under the back porch roof. She stepped outside and the wind caught her. Standing on her toes—she stopped.

A man sat a short bulldog mountain horse with a bald face. He simply sat there on his horse and nodded at her like he was taking her all in. A man she knew. She felt his stare and her heart quickened. Recalling the torrid time at the Peralta Springs that they'd had on the ground, she dried her sweaty palms on the side of her dress.

"You look like you've been surviving," he said, and then looked around from his horse at things.

"I lost some goats and sheep while I was gone. But I have shot two coyotes and they stay away now." She came off the porch holding up her dress tail. *Oh, God, make him get off the horse and hold me.*

"Get down and we'll put up your horse. It's safe. He won't be back for weeks. That's sure a nice horse," she said, admiring the animal.

"I traded for him in Mexico. He suited me."

With both hands, she held his left arm against her ripe pear-shaped breasts. Wanted him to know that under this dress there was a real woman. They headed for the corral, reins in her hand. She inspected his broad shoulders as he stripped off the saddle and pad.

Then he removed the bridle and turned the horse loose inside the pen.

"There's hay and water for him. He'll be fine for days in there—"

Her words were cut off by his hard kiss and he clutched her in his arms. Her brain swirled and she wanted more—lots more.

"I have bad news."

"Yes?"

"Ojo Nevado is dead."

She fought back tears and swallowed a knot. "I thought so—I mean I thought he was dead."

He pulled her to him and hugged her as she sobbed on his vest. With diamonds sparkling on her lashes, she wet her lips and stepped back. "Thank you. I am so grateful for your honesty about this matter. You knew. I never said . . ."

His powerful hand squeezed her shoulder and they headed for the house. "Now, what's the biggest problem you've got around here?"

"A coatimundi is eating my baby chickens."

He nodded as if in deep thought about the matter. "We'll get him tonight."

"Good. How are the rich women you went back to help?"

"They're probably buying steamer tickets right now to go see the world."

"Let me think. I saw Utah once, and Arizona getting here in a wagon, and Mexico off a horse. I don't want any steamer ticket. But-but you'll do any day."

He backed her against the wooden siding on the porch and kissed her again. Her knees about buckled when he reached inside her dress and his calloused hand cupped her right breast. Her breathing became impossible—oh.

Two weeks and three dead coatimundis later, Slocum stood waiting in Tucson for the stagecoach to load for Prescott. It would be lots cooler in the mountains.

Watch for

SLOCUM AND BELLE STARR

368th novel in the exciting SLOCUM series
from Jove

Coming in October!